STRAY ALLY

Book #1 in The Dog Complex Series

TROY LAMBERT

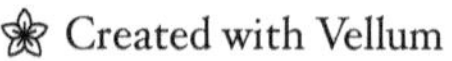 Created with Vellum

To my dog, Houston. You were my best friend for a long time, and have been gone for a while, but I still miss you. Here's hoping you are chasing a ball somewhere in doggie heaven, where there is no more doggie blindness and your nose is as strong as ever. To Indie, who followed Houston over the Rainbow Bridge, may you be able to fetch and swim as long as you want without tiring. I miss you.

CHAPTER ONE

"Mr. Clarke?"

"Speaking. Who's this?" I stood in my kitchen, sipping my morning coffee. I'd just returned from my daily run, had taken a shower, and was debating on what to do with the rest of my day. Forced retirement didn't suit me, and I needed more than hobbies to fill my time. I needed a job.

A bored ex-Marine was a dangerous thing.

"It's Adam Larson, IronClad Security."

"I've heard of you guys. What can I do for you?"

"I'm looking for some help. The new governor is having a rally soon, and we've been hired by Reverend Benjamin Wolfe to provide some additional security."

"Sounds easy enough."

"As you can understand," Adam continued. "Both the governor and the Reverend have received regular threats."

"I can't say that I am surprised in this state. Aryans?"

"Most, yes. It seems that not all of them left. I thought you might be a good fit because of your past experience."

"Most of my past experiences are classified, Mr. Larson."

"I don't know details. You were referred to me."

"By whom?"

"I can't say. Are you interested?"

"I'd be happy to come in and talk with you about it." I was interested, maybe. Even a boring security position beat staying at home trying to tend rose bushes and grown tomatoes. Still, it would depend on who I would be working with. IronClad had a great reputation. I just wanted to make sure they would live up to it.

"If things work out, this could turn into something more permanent. We could use a man with your skills."

Clarke didn't know if Larson meant that, or if he even knew what Clarke's skills were. He was a killer, a soldier who had gone too far more than once. True, the results had been good. Good until he was quietly chaptered out, that is.

I remember well. I love my wife, Marsha. My relatively new and quiet lifestyle.

But the warrior inside me only sleeps, and when it wakes...

When it wakes, people die. If I could do something, anything, that would keep that warrior in hibernation as long as possible, I'd feel much better about everything.

Private security might not be the answer, but it could be an answer. Maybe part of a wider solution.

"Does Monday morning work for you?"

"Shoot me an address, and I will be there." I answered.

———

THE SKATEBOARD COLLIDED with my windshield, and I braked with both feet, screeching forward. The body hit the glass next, spider-webbing it as the skater's helmet-clad head struck the glass in the center of my vision. The rear-view mirror separated from the window and hit the center of the seat with a thud as the car skidded to a stop.

Marsha is gonna be pissed, came the unbidden thought. *We just replaced this windshield.*

Where did he come from? Creedence still blared from the stereo speakers as I turned the ignition key off. Silence descended, broken a moment later by distant sirens.

I lifted my hand and felt wetness on my forehead, cut by— something. *Glass? Must have been.*

I opened the door, dazed. Under the helmet, a young face offered a blank stare. Nothing but blackness filled his eyes. Not good.

"You okay, kid?" I felt stupid asking. Stupider for expecting a response. "What were you doing on the freeway?"

I heard distant voices. Looked up. Kids, on the overpass above. *Did he fall?*

They pointed. One slugged the other one. A scuffle broke out and they ran. All of them.

The sirens came closer. Another car pulled up, tires squealing as it braked, rocking on its springs as it came to a stop.

"What happened? Is everyone okay?" the driver asked.

Struck dumb, I just pointed. The skateboard rested half on the roof, half on the shattered windshield. The skater lay below it, unmoving, his left foot against the hood ornament, the Mercedes star cocked sideways.

"Is he..?"

He didn't finish, but rushed over, feeling for a pulse, checking for breath. All things I should have done but for some reason couldn't. My training had not taken over.

He shook his head, glanced over at me. "What was he doing here?" I shrugged.

"Did you see him?"

Head wag, substituted for speech. "Are you okay?"

Another head wag. I couldn't articulate what was wrong. "You're bleeding."

I managed a nod, and then my legs gave out. I dropped to the pavement and grimaced as my tailbone impacted the hard surface. I heard a whimper. It must have been me, because the other driver rushed over.

I stared ahead, seeing and not seeing the scene. A combat veteran, I had killed before. But never a kid.

The sirens got closer, red and blue light illuminated Marsha's car, the body, the skateboard, the chrome of her wheels, even making the brake lights appear to flash.

Help arrived, even though the boy was clearly beyond help.

———

"TYLER? TYLER?" The cop shouted the name over and over. I didn't understand why. I watched, my mind far away.

Far away. "That's my boy! That's my boy! Tyler wake up! Wake up!"

The other driver tried to hold the cop back, but he kept shaking the skater.

The cop stopped shaking the boy. Distant wailing grew louder as other sirens approached. More help was arriving.

The stale unmoving air was reluctant to enter my lungs. I struggled for oxygen in silence. Then his eyes met mine. The other driver tried to stop him, I'll give him that. But he couldn't. I couldn't stop myself. He came at me.

He came at me.

"You killed my boy!" His shout filled my world, shattering the bubble I'd been in. "You piece of shit, you killed my boy!"

"Stop!" A voice, the Good Samaritan driver.

The cop launched himself at me, hands outstretched, as if to strangle me.

My body didn't consult my brain. It rose from its sitting position in one smooth motion. As the incensed father approached, it moved on its own, spun away from him, struck him on the back as he roared by, increased his momentum, and watched as he fell awkwardly onto the asphalt. He wasn't done.

I'd killed his boy.

He rushed back at me, and my body once again responded as I had trained it to. All of those hours. Strike, twist, pull, strike.

My fist impacted his side, then his chest. My foot lashed out, struck his knee with an audible crunch. He half fell again and drew his gun.

Another cruiser rolled onto the scene. An ambulance.

A fire truck.

A supervisor. EMTs.

Model citizens.

They all saw me do it.

He raised the gun. I spun inside his aim. My hands went to work, striking his wrist, breaking it.

Grabbing the gun. Turning it in my hand. Firing. Not once, but twice.

Double tap. Fighting like I was trained. Just like that, I was a cop killer. Correction.

I killed a cop's son. Then I killed a cop.

Self-defense sure, but unreasonable force used in response to a threat. And I was trained.

There went any chance a new job opportunity.

———

"HE SLID THE RAIL, halfway. We did it all the time." Stephen said.

"That's when he fell." Mr. Jeffers, the prosecuting attorney stated.

"Yeah. I tried to grab him, but he went over the edge. Landed on that Mercedes."

"Then what?"

"The driver got out. Walked away and stared. Like he was in shock or something."

"Another driver pulled up?"

"Objection, leading the witness." Mr. Rockford, attorney for the defense, stood.

"Overruled."

"Thank you, your Honor. Go ahead, Stephen."

"Yeah. Anyway, then the other dude pulled up. He went and checked Tyler over, then shook his head."

"He was dead?"

"Objection again your Honor. The witness is not a medical professional, and he was thirty feet above the victim at the time, on an overpass. How could he know if the victim was dead or not?"

"Your Honor, may the prosecution approach?" Mr. Jeffers seemed flustered.

"Both of you, my chambers, five minutes." He stood and exited. The bailiff led them back.

"Gentlemen?" The judge glared at both attorneys.

"Your Honor, the defense would like to stipulate some things are just facts," Mr. Rockford began.

"Like?"

"The defense would like to stipulate that the boy was dead when he struck the car. We are trying to prove that he was dead before he struck the car, but for brevity with these witnesses we are willing to stipulate that at the time they saw the boy on the hood of the car, after he fell, he was indeed dead."

"Mr. Jeffers?"

"The prosecution is reluctant your Honor. We know that by the time the second driver arrived on the scene, the witnesses had fled, the boy was dead. As Mr. Clarke is not here to defend himself, we have no way of knowing if he checked the boy for a pulse, and if he was dead on impact, before impact, or a few moments after."

"Time of death testifies to cognizance and possible negligence," the Judge said.

"Exactly your Honor."

"Okay, overruled. Mr. Jeffers, quit trying to establish time of death with non- medical witnesses. On another note, Mr. Rockford, where is your client?"

"Whereabouts still unknown your Honor. We have our best

people on it, but as you know he disappeared shortly after his wife posted bail, and no one has seen him since."

"I'm sure you're trying your best. Jeffers?"

"Our best are on it too. There is an issue, your honor."

"Yes?"

"No one knows if Todd Clarke is indeed the defendant's name."

"What?"

"His army records are sealed. We have no access. He worked special ops for them, and there seems to be some rumor that his name was changed legally at some point."

"If his file is classified, I can't force the military to honor a subpoena. Mr. Rockford, can you answer me a question?"

"Yes, your Honor?"

"Who's paying your fees? I know you don't have to answer."

"I'm sure your Honor is aware of who the defendant's wife is, and who her father is."

"Are you saying..?"

"That's as far as I'll go your Honor. Attorney-client privilege."

"All right. Your client is still a wanted man."

"Understood your Honor."

"And you, Mr. Jeffers?"

"Yes, your Honor."

"Any new information comes directly to my office."

"Yes, Sir."

"Off the record." The court reporter stopped typing.

"You two play nice. I know your history. I don't give a shit. It doesn't belong in my courtroom, understood?"

Twin nods.

"Ten-minute recess. I gotta piss. I'll see you inside."

Both men filed out, not speaking. Rockford turned left, pulling out his phone. Time to make a call.

CHAPTER TWO

*W*here are you from, Private?
    Idaho, Sir.
        You the what? Where did you say?
Idaho, Sir.
That's right, you look like the ho. You're pretty. I like you.
Sir...
What were you about to say to me Private?
Nothing, Sir.
Bullshit! Get on your face. Push until I get tired, and I just had a nap and coffee. Who the fuck is next?

No answer came from the rest of the platoon.

He did pushups rapidly, not even pacing himself. He could do a thousand pushups if he was ordered to.

From the corner, an Army sergeant wearing a maroon beret cocked sideways watched as the Marines trained. As the private did pushup after pushup, not even breaking a sweat, a small smile formed at the corners of his lips.

THE WATER ROARED BY, mere feet away. Rafters would soon

decorate the floor of the canyon, and it would be better if I was higher up in the woods or asleep in the cave by the time they floated by.

I dropped and did thirty pushups in rapid succession to warm up. I didn't want to start a fire that morning. The sky looked good. Maybe thunderstorms in the afternoon, but that wouldn't be a problem.

I looked around. There was some risk in leaving gear there, but it was small. Several caves dotted the rock face, and the likelihood that any hiker or rafter would pick that one to explore, especially deep enough to find my temporary home was next to zero. Occasionally I would come back to find they had taken a piss, or worse a shit, just inside the opening, but I endured it because it deterred others from exploring deeper.

I peered at the wall. I made the tick marks there with black marker. Floor to ceiling. Eighty-seven kills I knew about. Others I could assume, but my mind embraced absolutes. It liked solid numbers, hard facts.

Since I was wanted, the time had come to balance Karma or risk eternal damnation. I knew where I should start.

While climbing the hill, I swapped the batteries in the satellite phone with the ones in the solar charger. The latest military technology. Stolen, of course.

Shouldering my backpack, I started to jog. It was three miles to the lookout, and I wanted to be there by nine.

———

HE ANSWERED THE PHONE. "Go for Anderson."

"Rockford, Colonel. Any news?"

"None."

"Nothing?"

"Negative contact. I told you the boy is good."

"You also said he's crazy."

"Medical discharge. Mentally unstable, yes. But that doesn't erase his training."

"You'll let me know."

"You have no idea, Rockford. This last thing may have pushed him over the edge. Either he'll disappear forever, or when he surfaces..." The colonel's voice trailed off.

"Yes?"

"When he surfaces, everyone will know."

———

THOU SHALT NOT KILL.

Not the clearest commandment, it actually refers only to murder.

What I was planning wasn't murder. It was war.

War was what I trained for. Step one.

Adequately arm myself. I set up the satellite phone.

"Wilson." A familiar voice answered.

"Clarke."

"The usual package?"

"Roger that."

"Delivery?"

I gave him the coordinates. "I need wheels."

"Chevy or Ford?"

"Chevy."

"Riggins Park. Thursday. Keys at the hotel, usual spot."

"Thanks."

"Clarke?"

"Yeah?"

"Be careful."

I terminated the connection. Wilson knew this wasn't official, but he'd still get paid. I liked him. I hoped I wouldn't have to kill him.

———

"No, Sparky! Get your ass back here."

The dog ran forward anyway, barking. A man dressed in camouflage descended the outside stairs of the concrete building.

"Hey, Sparky, leave that man alone."

Sparky did not listen, his tail wagging in greeting.

Jesus, please, no. It was too late.

Why did you have to hike here today? I mentally shouted at the man. Outwardly, I smiled, and slowly stood. The sat phone still lay on the ground, fully assembled, including the signal scrambler. Even if he'd never seen this kind of set up before, he'd know this was something different.

The hike wasn't a short one either. You didn't forget people you met at the lookout. It was a weekday. Why couldn't it be empty?

"My name's Alan. How you doin'?" A definite drawl defined the man's speech. He held out his hand to shake.

"Todd Clarke." We shook. Alan was tall and thin but muscular.

"What you got there?" he asked.

"Sat phone."

"Pretty nice. Different than some of the ones I've seen. Didya rent it, or is it yours?"

I squatted down to pet Sparky as his owner talked. He looked to be a German Shepherd mix, similar to some of the dogs I had seen in the military. I scratched behind his ears.

Good dog. Good boy.

"It's mine," I answered.

"Wow. That musta set you back a pretty penny."

"Yeah. It's worth it though."

He looked me up and down, his smile fading. "So what're you doin' out here?"

"Just hiking."

"Where are you camped? I didn't see anyone else down by the lake."

"I hiked up from the canyon side this morning."

Please, stop asking questions.

"Huh." He seemed suddenly suspicious. On edge. I didn't have any options.

I scratched Sparky behind the ears again as I stood, but he sensed a change in the atmosphere too. The dog growled, low and questioning, in the back of his throat.

The best I could do was make it quick.

"Well, it was nice to meet you." I held out my hand this time. "Maybe I'll see you down by the lake later."

As he returned my handshake, I pulled him closer. In a single motion my left hand unsheathed my knife and shoved it dead center into his throat. A whoosh of air escaped as it severed his windpipe. Blood gushed, but I darted to the side. I leaned his head forward to minimize both the flow and the noise.

Sparky yelped in fear, and before I could lower his unfortunate master to the ground, he leapt at me, teeth bared. The world slowed down for a full minute. I didn't want to kill a dog.

I can't kill a dog.

My forearm struck the side of his head, sending him sprawling. He was agile, and rolling with the blow, he landed on his feet.

I dropped to all fours onto his level. Our eyes met. He growled again but didn't attack.

"Good boy," I cooed. "Good dog. I don't want to hurt you, boy." Studying me, he settled back on his haunches, still growling softly.

"C'mere boy." I held out my hand. "C'mere. I had to, boy. I'm sorry. I had to. That doesn't mean we can't be friends."

The growl slowly subsided, and the dog crawled forward slowly, licking his lips. "That's it. Good boy."

Not really in petting distance yet, he stretched out his nose and sniffed my hand. I let him and waited what seemed like a long time. Finally, I put my hand on top of his head and patted him, again scratching behind his ears, something he seemed to like.

He panted, and his dark brown eyes darted back and forth nervously. I eased forward, lowering myself to the stony ground. He crawled his way over next to me, and I pet him all over. Rolling to his back, he let me rub his belly.

I'd managed to make friends.

I slowly stood, and he stood with me. It was then I noticed a tag on his collar. I spun it around and looked.

Under the name "Sparky" engraved on the tag I read the name "Aston Lewis" with an address. I looked over at the body.

Hmm.

I moved over, rolling the man to his back and searching his pockets. Sparky sat a few feet away and whimpered.

He carried no wallet or ID.

He wasn't even carrying a bottle of water.

Maybe he left his pack in the lookout. You didn't need much to hike up from the camp below, but it promised to be a warm day. You'd want water with you at the very least.

I glanced again at Sparky. He wagged his tail and bobbed his head.

"Let's go," he seemed to say.

He didn't seem that attached to Alan. The action had scared him, but he had little loyalty to his "master.: That was unusual for any breed mixed with a Shepherd. They were fiercely loyal. I stood up and looked around. Something felt wrong.

I packed up the sat gear, shoving it in my pack, then grabbed the body and carried it to the lower part of the tower.

"Caution: Hantavirus Present. Do Not Enter," the sign on the door said. I eased it open and dropped the body inside. I pulled the door closed, ensuring the latch clicked into place, trying not to imagine what the rats and other critters would do to Alan, if that was the man's name. It could be months before it was discovered. Maybe never, unless someone came searching for him.

I ascended the stairs to the lookout proper. Inside I saw an oddly familiar pack. Glimpsed a sat phone. Not as sophisticated as the one I had, but military for sure. Next to the pack sat a compact case. A .22 rifle with a small scope sat on the table. I picked it up. It wasn't a sniper rifle, but at a reasonably close range it would do some damage. But probably not kill.

Alan wasn't a hunter. Hunting season was months away, and there was almost nothing you could hunt here with that small caliber rifle. It was time to go.

I took the rifle but left the pack and the case. I peered inside first, removing two extra clips of ammunition I found there. They would be enough to get me out of the mountains. Unless Alan wasn't alone.

"C'mon Sparky, let's go." I took off at a brisk pace. The dog kept up, even running ahead of me at times. He might have proved useful if he stuck around, even if for nothing more than warning me of coming danger.

I would find him some food and treats in Riggins. In the meantime, maybe I could catch him a fish or two.

Tonight, we'd head out, under the cover of darkness. I'd left a couple of things back at the cave I needed to pick up. Adjusting the pack on my back, I increased my walk to a jog.

———

"ANDERSON."

"Colonel, we've lost coms with your man in the woods."

"How long is he overdue?"

"Two hours."

"Fuck!"

"What do you want us to do, Colonel?"

"What assets do you have?"

"I have a team on standby. Four hours to the area, then they would have to find him."

"He'll be gone by then."

"Can I make a suggestion, Colonel?"

"Sure."

"There are only two quick ways to get out of that wilderness. I can split the team and cover them both."

"If he takes another way?"

"It will take him longer, and we won't find him anyway."

"Okay, try it."

"Yes, Sir."

"I want to know as soon as anyone on your team spots him."

"Roger that, Sir."

The Colonel terminated the connection and leaned back in his chair. No matter how he looked at things, this was not good news.

Todd Clarke was one of the most dangerous men he knew. He was also the smartest. And one of the craziest. If he snapped...

Colonel Anderson had no illusions about how Clarke felt about him. He stared out his window and wondered if he was doing the right thing.

———

THE TEMPERATURE FELL with the darkness. I zipped the legs back on to my hiking pants and pulled my fleece over my head. I glanced over at Sparky.

Lapping cool water from the stream, he stared back at me. I filtered my water, and only just pumped enough to fill my Camelback. I'd planned to go the short way, cutting over the goat trail past Sheep Lake.

Go the long way.

Sparky stared at me, and at the same time, I heard the voice in my head.

Go the long way.

It's nine more fucking miles. The voice of logic spoke up, and I wanted to listen to it.

I stopped prepping my pack, stopped doing anything. Sparky still stared at me, and when I looked at him, his tail wagged.

Probably fucking hungry, I told myself.

I'd forgotten about getting Sparky a fish or two. Poor thing needed the energy for the hike.

Especially if we were going to hike even farther.

The voice was right, be it dog or the beginning stages of insanity. If Alan wasn't alone, or even if he was, and someone was expecting him to contact them, if they came looking, the Goat Pass would be the route they'd take. They'd never expect him to go around.

I dug in my pack for some precious jerky. I held a piece back for me and tossed two at Sparky. I'd get some more at the rendezvous tonight. There was an all-night gas station near there.

The moon rose over the horizon. With it shining, and the help of my stolen night vision goggles, we'd made good time.

The dog could keep up.

"Time to go." I whistled. Sparky wagged his tail and took the lead down the trail as if he knew exactly where we were going.

Nine miles is nothing.

Shut the fuck up, I told myself.

I set off at a grueling but sustainable pace. Sparky led most of the time.

CHAPTER THREE

*C*ome on soldier! Come on!
> *Move your ass!*
>> *Are you quitting on me?*

No, Sir!

It looks like you are quitting!

No, Sir!

Then move it!

He forced his feet to push forward, faster and faster. Mile seventeen. A simple twenty miler today. He knew he was in the "A" group. For some reason, though, they wouldn't stop pushing him.

So he did the only thing he knew how. He worked harder, walked faster, ran faster, did more pushups.

Still, they never let up.

They didn't know he'd already spotted the guy watching his training. Army puke.

They lost. He'd joined the Marines when the Army had rejected him and removed him from training.

"Mental health issues," they'd used as their reason.

Bullshit.

The Marines loved his attitude.

They accepted him. For the first time in years, someone accepted him for who he was. Then they started to mold him. Already the toughest motherfucker he knew, the Marines made him harder.

And harder.

The only voices he heard were his Drill Instructors and he was happy to listen to them. They hadn't told him to kill.

Yet.

If they did, he would listen.

Private Alec Norwood had killed before.

No one knew either. Besides being a tough motherfucker, Alec was already the killer the Marines wanted to mold him into.

And a damn good one.

———

"Get up there, soldier."

"Sorry, Sir. It's the altitude."

"Well, the altitude ain't gonna affect Clarke, and he ain't waitin' for us, that's for sure."

"Yes, Sir."

The staggered line of soldiers worked its way up the goat trail and over the pass. Below to the left on the way up spread a great view of Mirror Lake, and as they crested the ridge, the wooded shore of Sheep Lake came into view. Sergeant Abrams raised his binoculars and surveyed the inlet creek and the incoming trail. No movement. To the south was a single campfire. Otherwise, the shoreline was empty.

He knew of two other ways out of the wilderness. They seemed unlikely choices. He'd been ordered to wait in the campground, but Colonel Anderson wasn't really in charge of his unit. In this case, he could intercept Clarke if he tried to come out this way.

And flank him if he went the other. It seemed like that would be the plan.

He'd served with Clarke once, just before the Army discharged for him being too batshit even for black ops.

He hadn't been on the team that had found the bodies, but he'd heard the rumors. It didn't make him nervous. He and his men were at least as badass as Clarke. They would have the advantage of surprise. There was no way he could know they were behind him. Hell, he couldn't even know they were coming. Even if he'd captured Duyon, which was unlikely in itself; and made him talk, even more unlikely; he didn't even know they were planning this.

It had been his idea for Duyon to take Lewis's dog, to look even more like just another day hiker.

Dogs made good warning systems.

They headed down, circling the lake, headed for the trail. The men weren't breathing quite as hard now.

If they found this stretch hard, he dreaded their reaction to part two of the hike. The next section would require stealth, too. He had no desire to tip off Clarke. God only knew what would happen if he spotted them on his tail.

———

THEY'RE COMING BEHIND YOU.

Sparky stared at me, and I swore I heard his voice in my head. Another person might have asked who was following, but I knew.

Soldiers.

I'd thought I would start the war, but someone wanted to start early. No problem.

I didn't have much with me, but it would be plenty. How many could they send?

No more than a squad, the voice told me. I nodded. After all, I was only one guy.

Although they'd seen what I could do, they continued to underestimate me. I didn't mind that at all.

I remembered Sparky barking at me in greeting the first time we met, just hours ago, and I smiled. I scratched his ear quickly, and he responded with a short bark.

It was a good spot to set up a trap, about a half mile of flat before the climb out started. If they were going to try to flank me, I might as well know how far they were behind, and I could take out one or two in the process.

Inventorying the contents of my pack, the extra ammo for the rifle and additional tent stakes seemed like a meager stash, but they'd have to do. My hands set about doing what they'd been trained to.

What I was wired to do.

It was dark. There would be some great spots to set traps on the way up too. "Me and you, Sparky, me and you."

I killed a boy and a cop. They were innocent, and it really wasn't my fault. But they were just the latest in the long list of many.

Don't forget Alan.

Sparky cocked his head. *Yeah, but I don't think he was one of the innocent ones.* He padded around and watched with interest as I dug two holes, about twenty yards apart, for the first ambush. He even tried to help dig, before I pushed him away with a content smile.

———

THE LEAD SOLDIER held his fist in the air. *Halt.*

They all did.

He waved his arms, palms facing the ground.

Get down.

They obeyed, each pointing their weapons outward. Known as a field of fire, each man was assigned a twenty-degree fan in front or to the side of their position to cover. The men in the rear covered that area: no one could sneak up behind them.

Abrams moved forward. "What's going on?"

"Rock carron. Could it be an I.E.D? Another kind of trap?"

"What would he make an I.E.D. with? A fucking fish? We're in the middle of nowhere, and while you fuck around looking for an ambush from a guy who can't possibly know we're coming, he's making time and getting away."

"Yes, Sir."

"Now move these men out."

He waved his arms, palms up. The squad rose as one.

A circular motion with his forearm, his finger pointed straight up, followed by a forward waving motion got the men moving.

Abrams heard a whistling sound pass his ear and then the crack of a small arms rifle. The lead man dropped, and a second shot sounded. The injured man screamed and grasped at his ear, where blood flowed like a swollen stream in springtime.

"Down! Down!"

The men dropped and faced outward. Another shot, and one soldier returned fire. As soon as the first man fired, all the guns on his side joined in.

"Cease fire! Cease fire!" Abrams exploded with anger. The gunfire stopped.

"Where are your targets? What are you aiming at?"

"Just returning fire, Sir!" One man shouted.

"Returning what fire? Do you have eyes on a target?"

"No, Sir." The return shout was more subdued.

"Then stop wasting your ammo. That goddamn guy isn't even here, I bet."

"But Sir..."

"Fan out. Search for booby traps."

"He shot Ellery."

"Lucky, that's all. That wasn't a well-aimed shot."

"How do you know that Sir?"

"If Clarke was actually pulling the trigger, Ellery would be dead. Patch him up. We move in five."

———

I HEARD THE GUNFIRE. Good.

And bad. They'd already reached the first trap. I increased my pace as much as I dared in the dark. I needed to be enough ahead of them to collect my goods and get out of town. Originally, I'd planned to spend the night, get some breakfast in the morning, and then split. One more night's sleep would do me good.

But they brought the fight to me.

Take it to them. Kill. Kill.

Kill.

The voice belonged to me, chanting in my head, filling my ears.

Kill. Sparky looked at me and sprinted ahead. He seemed to sense my thoughts.

He whined, begged me to follow. They say sometimes animals are strangely in tune with human emotions and thoughts, especially when they're close to their owners.

He's not even my dog.

Maybe he's your dog, or kind of destined to be.

I don't believe in destiny.

Yeah, but maybe the dog does.

It was no time to dwell on stray thoughts. I needed to move out, set up the last trap. As the saying went, I had miles to go before I could sleep.

I uncoiled the rope as I walked, the rifle slung loosely over my shoulder. Up ahead, I saw Sparky running back my direction, and it made me genuinely happy.

———

I HEARD them before I saw them. They were good. Sparky growled in the back of his throat.

Quiet.

He cocked his head, listening. His lips twitched over his teeth, but he didn't make another sound.

I'd thought an order for him to be quiet, and he'd obeyed. I didn't have to say a thing.

A branch moved. Then another. A shadow filled an area of light, and then passed by.

My breath slowed to its regular rhythm just in time. The trap was barely set, the risk of discovery high. The rope was set tight, but not too tight. Patience would bring satisfaction.

I counted. One, two, three. Four, there. Three more followed. That seemed to be all. Seven survived the first trap, or at least seven of them still moved. Two injured, one man with each to guard them, and one—where? He'd spotted a dozen to start with.

They were only two switchbacks away. Time grew short. There, at the end. Two men walking so close together they looked like one.

My rifle was pointed toward the trail, safety off, steadied on a boulder. One smooth motion would bring it to bear.

And the dog?

Stay boy. Wait. I thought it, and the dog obeyed.

Sparky lay down and placed his head on his front paws. His eyes remained alert, pointed ears perked at every sound.

But he stayed. Just like I told him.

Good boy.

His tail wagged, once.

Shaking my head, I turned my attention back to the trail. Fifty yards. Forty. Thirty. I smelled them.

Heard the rustle of their clothing.

The clatter of fasteners and firearms as they made their way cautiously forward.

Not.

Quite.

Yet.

I stopped breathing. Stopped moving. Watched the mark.

It was funny how they keyed in on the one thing that didn't matter, missed the one that did.

Three. Two. One.

I pulled the rope, the clatter started, and they turned to stare. Logs rolled down the rocky slope.

The first log struck, a small pine, but it was enough. The first man fell, his finger tightening on the trigger of his weapon, bullets chasing each other into the sky.

The second man tried to dodge, but too late. I heard a crunch as his leg bent backward at a horrifying angle.

The third fired absurdly at the log rolling his way.

It bounced off a rock at the last second, and he nearly ducked out of its path, but it struck his forehead, and he flipped backward off the steep trail into the forest below.

Stones and debris followed the logs. A small avalanche raced down the slope. Those in its way didn't stand a chance.

Two more soldiers discharged their weapons, unsure of how to combat this force of nature. I saw four and five go down in a hail of boulders and gravel. Dust obscured my vision.

As it cleared I saw number six trying to scramble out of the way, but number seven pushed him into the flow, using him like a shield as he danced to the side. He bounded back down the trail, and remained still behind a boulder for another thirty seconds or so, until the rock slide stopped.

Sparky barked once, sharply.

"Quiet!" I whispered. Or thought. It was hard to tell. "Clarke?" A familiar voice called. It belonged to Sergeant Grier Abrams.

I knelt, resting the rifle on a boulder, taking careful aim. I didn't answer. "Clarke, I hear you have the dog. Unless you took up barking, you bitch."

I squeezed the trigger but intentionally aimed low. It was the only answer he'd get from me.

"Oh close," he said. "Don't want to kill me yet? Want to hear what I have to say?"

Silence.

"Where's Duyon? Did you kill him?"

I fired again, high this time.

"Missed? I don't think so. You're better than that. Here Sparky!" he called. Sparky sat up, recognizing the voice.

"Stay boy," I encouraged.

"He speaks! They're coming for you, Clarke. You shouldn't have killed that cop. And that kid? Terrible accident. Hard to live with that one, eh?"

The dog barked.

"Here, boy. Want a biscuit?" Sparky sprinted off in his direction. It set me off.

I fired.

One, chest. Two, Shoulder. Three, kneecap.

Then I stood and chased my dog toward him. I hoped he wasn't dead, and really did have biscuits in his pockets.

———

"WILSON."

"Clarke here."

"You got some heat, man."

"Yeah."

"Whatcha need? Did I miss somethin' in the supplies?"

"I need somebody to watch my dog."

"Didn't know you had a goddamn dog."

"I don't. I mean, didn't. I acquired one recently."

"A stray? Leave it behind. Better yet, put it down. There're a lot of dogs in the world. I can get you a great one when you are clear of this. My uncle breeds Labs. You can't go wrong with a Lab."

"Can't. I guess I'll get all the stuff I need at the next pet supply store."

"Don't tell me you are going on the run with a dog?"

I glanced at Sparky, sitting calmly in the passenger seat. "Not running, Wilson."

"You mean?"

"Yeah. It's time to finish this. I planned to take the fight to them, but they're chasing me now."

"Dogs make good alarms. What kind is he?"

"A Shepherd mix. He already earned his keep. I'm leaving Riggins now. I need a hidey-hole for a few days."

"I got just the place. Head east. Sending you the coordinates now."

"Thanks Wilson."

"Clarke?"

"Yeah?"

"Good luck with the dog."

"Thanks."

I glanced in the back as I slid in. Abrams was bleeding, but not too bad. His wild eyes looked at me over the duct tape. I harbored no illusions of using him as a hostage, and he knew it. He was nothing to me but a source of information.

That's why he was so scared.

Sparky looked at him, barked and growled. "Good dog," I said, meaning it.

I shifted the Chevy into gear and glanced at the burner phone Wilson provided me. Things just got better and better. It had GPS and everything. A second later, it lit up with a text message containing coordinates. I glanced at them, recognizing the place. Leave it to Wilson to direct me to the best accommodations.

"Get comfortable Abrams. I'd tell you to hang on, but..." I laughed. I heard muffled grunts from behind the tape.

No need to turn on the radio. I wouldn't get even the strongest stations out here. Sparky lay contentedly on the seat, his head in my lap.

I whistled as I drove away.

Seven confirmed dead. I mentally put them in the positive column. *Karma, I'm going to even the scales.*

———

He answered the phone on the first chirp. "Anderson."

Listened for a second. "Slow down Sheriff. Where did you pick them up?"

"I see. Who knows about this?"

"Keep it quiet. No press. I'll be on scene in an hour maximum. Can you hold it in your pants that long?"

He laughed at the answer. "No disrespect intended. Hang in there. The good guys are on the way."

The disadvantage of these new phones. You couldn't slam them into the cradle. Four men alive. Two of those injured. The other seven dead. One missing. Who was missing? *If it's fucking Abrams, I'm going to kill him myself if he survives.*

He glanced at the clock. Eight a.m. When did the attack happen? How much of a head start did this asshole have on him and his men?

It seemed dainty and unmanly to slide his finger across the screen and punch in a few numbers, but such was the way of the new world. He wanted to pound buttons.

"We have a chopper on standby, right?"

"Roger," replied the voice on the other end.

"Five minutes. Full of fuel."

"Destination?"

"Idaho County Sheriff's office. Then maybe a flyover of Seven Devils."

"Sir..."

"Just get that bird in the air. I want the goddamn rotors turning in one."

"Yes, Sir."

He missed the old army days, when he could bust an NCO to Private for looking at him wrong.

Clarke was supposed to be eliminated by now, an easy thing to do to a man behind bars. But he'd jumped bail, and then dodged Plan B. Now Plan C. It was time to pull out all the stops and kill this motherfucker.

The time had come to move forward. Sometimes to move

forward you had to take care of the past. That way, those mistakes could never meander into the future.

I should have taken care of him long ago, when I had him in my sights. Ah well. The bastard would be in his sights one more time.

This time he wouldn't miss.

CHAPTER FOUR

*H*ow *would you like to do something special, Private Norwood?*

What would that be, Sir?

Maybe something more suited to your talents.

My talents, Sir?

Are you a killer Alec?

Sir? He trembled. Had they found out somehow?

A killer. You want to kill, don't you Private?

Yes, Sir.

You want to take out the enemy, hit him where he lives?

Yes, Sir.

It might be dangerous.

Of course, Sir.

It means more training. More money too.

I'm okay with that, Sir.

You have any family, Alec?

No, Sir.

They already knew that. They didn't know his father's death hadn't been an accident. This didn't seem like the time to discuss it.

The beret-wearing soldier swung at him.

Alec reacted, not even thinking about rank. He blocked the punch, and ducked inside the soldier's reach, striking him once in the chest, moving for another blow. A second later, he found himself on the ground.

A deep throated laugh sounded from behind him. "Not bad. We'll train you to be better."

He picked himself up.

I'm good with that.

Then come with me.

Don't I have to sign out?

You're already signed out. Let's go, Specialist.

But...

You got promoted too.

He followed the man out of the courtyard to a waiting Humvee.

———

"WAKE UP, WAKE UP!"

He was pale, much worse for the ride on the rutted road.

I pulled back the duct tape. There was no reason to leave it in place here.

The spartan compounds once active with Aryan Nations members sat abandoned all over the central wilderness of the state. Some locations were secret, unless you had dealt with the group in some retail capacity, the way they financed their operations. They often offered drugs or more frequently weapons. After a severe internal struggle and the formation of splinter groups in 1998 and the death of the primary leaders Richard Butler and Harold Ray Redfeairn passed away in 2003 and 2004, many members fled to Ohio or Arkansas. Although the barrack accommodations for the soldiers were basic at best, the leaders often had elaborate headquarters bunkers constructed on site.

Not only were they comfortable, but they had great security. The muffled sound of a 60K Ultra Quiet generator hardly vibrated the walls and provided ample light and power for more devices than I would ever need in the short time I'd planned to be there. The most important thing it powered was the alarm.

"Fucker!" He spat the word at me.

Opening a bottle of water, I smiled down at him. "Thirsty?"

Sparky barked.

"Oh, you too?" I spun the cap off the bottle and tipped it up to the dog. His tongue lapped thirstily at the contents, catching most of the water, but causing some to spatter to the floor.

"I don't have time to play games, Abrams. You know I won't let you live. I can do this easy or hard. You give me information, I kill you quick. Maybe you even get a final drink, even a hearty last meal."

"Clarke, please."

"This isn't about my fugitive status as a bail jumper. Why are they after me?"

"What makes you think I know?"

A swift kick to the man's gut caused the air to rush from his lungs, and he bent as much as his bonds would allow.

"No time for games, remember?"

"Maybe I just don't like you, and I'm after you for the personal satisfaction." The next kick broke Abrams' nose. He howled in pain as blood spurted and formed a new pattern on what I assumed was a pricey area rug.

"I'm not going to say a word," he gasped. "If you're going to kill me, just do it."

Control. A calm voice spoke in my head, but I could feel a buzzing starting in the back of my brain, near where it and the spinal cord met. It raced forward, threatening to take over.

Sparky barked sharply. The buzzing retreated. He nuzzled my hand, which had formed into a hard fist. I opened it, and patted his head, and he buzzing dulled further.

Think.

Good advice, coming from the dog by my side.

Glancing around, I spotted an old-style wooden rocker. It would do, so I pulled it over.

I picked Abrams up by the back of the collar and set him in it, pinning his hands behind him against the back of the chair. He moaned. It had to hurt, but I heard dread under the pain.

I ran a piece of fresh duct tape around his chest, securing him in position. Spread his legs, strapped each one to the rocker supports on either side. Tested the chair, rocking it back and forth. He couldn't move, but the chair moved nicely.

I know you are a nice dog, but can you act mean? I shot the thought at the dog, hoping the telepathy really worked.

A single sharp bark. *Does that mean yes? Are you a cat?*

Two sharp barks. Okay, that settled that. Abrams looked nervously at the dog.

"What's the matter? Not an animal lover?"

"Clarke, he's trained to..."

"To what?"

He shook his head. "Sic?"

Sparky growled and nipped toward Abrams exposed crotch. Teeth bared, foam gathered at the edge of his lips, he looked vicious.

"No! No!" Abrams tried to rock back, to flee, but his actions only set him rocking back and forth, each forward motion bringing him closer to Sparky's snapping jaws. I started to wonder if the dog meant it.

"Okay, okay, call him off! Jesus!"

"Sparky, sit."

Instantly the dog stopped barking and settled back on his haunches, watching me.

"I don't know how you made friends with that fucking dog so quick. He liked us, but he never really listened to anyone but Lewis."

"Huh. I'll file that in my 'I don't give a fuck file' for the moment. Who's behind this?"

"I can't..."

A low growl from Sparky, unbidden. *Damn, that dog is smart.*

"Clarke, this is big. You were set up, yeah. They tried to send you somewhere you'd be easier to neutralize."

"Like jail?"

"Yeah."

"So the arrest was a set up?"

"The arrest? Jesus, the whole thing."

"What do you mean?"

"How did all of this start?"

We were interrupted by the familiar whump of chopper rotors. Close. Time to go. Thinking suddenly took a back seat. Far back.

The buzzing started up again at the back of my brain, but this time Sparky didn't bark. Not a peep. The warrior living in me took over.

The dog followed at heel as I raced to the back of the building. "Clarke! Clarke!" I heard Abrams' cries, and had no compassion.

"Fuck you, Clarke!" Those would be his last words. It was time to blow this joint.

————

"There. See the truck?"

"I thought your guy was on foot?"

"Any stolen cars reported in the last few hours, Sheriff?"

"No, Sir."

"Then he has help."

"How do you know it's even him? People come to these abandoned places all the time. They're popular camp spots now."

"We're gonna find out in a few minutes. Do you have any men on the ground?"

"A few. I can call in Search and Rescue."

"How long?"

"Two hours to muster all of them."

"Okay, never mind. Anywhere we can land?" he asked the pilot.

"About a mile away. Tight clearing, Colonel, but I can do it."

"What are you waiting for?"

The pilot grinned.

Colonel Anderson looked around at the four exhausted soldiers. He didn't like their chances, and almost told the pilot to split.

Just then the chopper banked hard right and dropped to what seemed like inches above the trees. A minute later, it rose about twenty feet, and then executed a stomach-turning drop into a small clearing, the rotors narrowly missing the trees that skirted it. As the blades slowed, the soldiers disembarked, forming a loose guard at the four points of the compass. The colonel exited last. He waved a radio at the pilot.

"We'll be on the usual frequency. Keep it warm."

"Yes, Sir. Will we have any additional passengers on takeoff?"

"Not this time. Once we get him, we'll leave the body behind."

———

POWER DOWN THE GENERATOR. Unplug and cut back the wire leading to the house. Reverse the leads. Head inside. Cut the main wire leading into the breaker box. Cut the conduit and the wires leading out. Splice them together.

Go to the kitchen. Unhook the propane lines going to the stove. Take a deep breath. No smell. It must be off, but hopefully the tank isn't empty. Worries for later.

Go out front. Move the truck down the drive, hope I have time. The chopper landed a few minutes ago.

My body ran on automatic. The warrior in my head told my limbs, my fingers what to do. They responded like a well-oiled machine.

I ran back to the bunker, the dog my silent companion.

Reconnect the generator. Fire it up.

Sparks flew almost immediately. A fire started inside.

The distant screams belonged to Abrams. The warrior did not care, did not pause.

Spot the propane tank out back. A jog, and several taps down the side. A little in the bottom. Enough. Turn the lever on the outlet line. Smoke rolls out the stone framed windows, licking hungrily at the iron bars.

Run to the north. Hide behind the concrete barracks there.

Hear and feel the deep throb of the explosion. Taste the rotten egg residual of leaking propane. Hear the stones hitting the side of the barracks. Peek around. The top of the bunker is gone, and there's no more screaming.

———

THE LEAD SOLDIER held up his hand in the halt signal. The sound assaulted their ears just before they saw the rising smoke. The flames were barely visible, so the explosion must have been contained. The Sheriff jumped.

"Told you it was him. Stay next to me," the Colonel stated.

They remained stationary for only a moment, and then the leader motioned them forward. The explosion wasn't an immediate threat.

Colonel Anderson smiled to himself. He'd trained these men well. They knew that to wait too long here meant his wrath. Whatever they might be walking into, the men feared his wrath more. Things were just as they should be.

By his guess they were about halfway to the compound he'd spotted. No doubt Clarke would have surprises waiting for them. With little warning, they might get the jump on him if he was still there. By the sound of the explosion, he doubted it. He couldn't have a clue what was really going on, and until he did, Clarke would run.

At least he hoped so.

———

I HEADED NORTH FURTHER, spotting a trail in the direction the chopper landed, and headed down it.

Sparky stepped in front of me and gave two sharp barks.

No.

"Move mutt."

Two sharp barks.

"What the hell?"

Two sharp barks. He turned away from me.

Three sharp barks followed that seemed somehow amplified by the night which he followed with three long howls then three more sharp barks.

It couldn't be, but it sounded like Morse code. SOS in dog speak.

There was a ten second pause that seemed like it lasted forever.

Three sharp barks, three long howls answered, followed again by three sharp barks.

Another pause. Then a sudden cacophony of howls and barks rose from the woods.

The dog turned and looked at me.

He barked twice, and ran toward where I parked the truck. He trotted back and looked at me. One sharp bark.

Yes.

Follow him.

The warrior in me connected with the dog, spoke, and I obeyed.

I broke into a trot as the howls and barks became threatening growls behind me, moving away from us.

Sparky had called an S.O.S. into the woods and set up the perfect distraction. He seemed to be directing my escape.

I opened the driver's door of the truck and he jumped in first, moving all the way over to the passenger side. I hopped in behind him and started the engine.

He looked right in my eyes, and barked twice.

"Yes, let's go," I answered, and patted his head.

He wagged his tail. I exited the formerly gated compound, and headed east, deeper into the wilderness.

The woods came alive around us.

————

YELLOW EYES STARED at his every move. Something panted right behind him. Something was there; he didn't even have to look. He was half mile away from the chopper, and safety. He ran, his breath coming in ragged gasps, legs on fire with every step.

Tripping over a root, his arms spun for balance. He grabbed at a tree for support, a weak young sapling. It bent under his weight, slowing his fall, whipping from his hand as he released it. As his palm brushed a fallen log, a splinter pushed deep into it, causing him to cry out.

A bark followed by a growl sounded, close. Too close.

Picking himself up, he continued to run. *Were the others with him?*

He didn't care. Colonel Anderson possessed a well-founded fear of canines, and panic took over his mind.

There it was. The chopper. He crossed the clearing and leapt inside. Safe.

"Chief, get this bird in the air!" No response.

"Chief?"

He crawled forward.

The pilot's throat was torn wide open, canine teeth marks surrounding the wound, blood saturating the front of his uniform. From behind him, he heard a deep growl. Pulling his sidearm he turned to face his worst fear.

"Sergeant Norwood."

"Yes, Sir."

"You've described to this board the events of the evening of September 29. Do you attest that your account is true and complete to the best of your knowledge?"

"Yes, Sir."

"You realize that your conduct, while effective, was not in line with the mission and the mission objectives, and that such actions in other contexts might put in jeopardy the relationship between the United States and other nations?"

"Yes, Sir, I do."

He wanted to lash out, to explain, but the time for that was past. He couldn't tell them the truth: when crisis hit, the warrior in his head started to speak, and he had to obey. Had to.

The United States put the warrior there. They trained him to kill, without compulsion, without warning, without remorse.

"The board has no choice, Sergeant. You will be demoted from the rank of E-6 to E-5. You will receive a general discharge. Until such time as you can complete the exit process, you will be relieved of all duties, and will report to battalion sick call daily until your paperwork is complete."

"Yes, Sir."

"Do you have anything to say for yourself, Norwood?"

The decision he made at that moment changed his life forever. "No, Sir," he replied.

"Dismissed."

Norwood snapped a salute. Did an about face and exited into the bright sunshine.

He didn't get more than a dozen steps before a man in a black suit stopped him. "Alec Norwood?"

"Excuse me. I'm kind of occupied."

"Too occupied for a job offer?"

"I'm listening."

"Agent Rivas, FBI. Want to go for a drink?"

"Sure."

They shook hands, and the man gestured to a waiting sedan.

———

I RUBBED at the stump of the ring finger on my left hand as I drove.

It was a nervous tick I rarely noticed about myself, but one that Marsha pointed out all the time.

"Stop it!" I could hear her say.

"Stop what?"

"Rubbing your finger like that."

"I don't have a finger there."

"You know what I mean. Stop it!"

"Sorry." I tried stop. But when someone pointed my missing digit out I was oddly compelled to keep rubbing. I smiled at the memory.

A double bark interrupted my thoughts.

"Are you telling me to stop?"

One bark. *Yes.*

This can't be happening. I'm not talking to a dog.

Like without him around you are any saner?

I wondered what Marsha was doing right now. I wanted to call her, but knew the risk that would bring to both of us.

My thumb wandered over my stump again as I drove.

Sparky barked twice.

Now the dog was channeling my wife.

I stopped rubbing by putting both hands on the wheel. The road ended at a "T" and I took a left. North. Deeper into the woods.

I knew a good, defensible place.

If whoever decided to chase me keeps coming, they'd better bring an army.

———

WHEN THE DOG saw the gun, it jumped from the chopper before Colonel Anderson could fire. He fired anyway, into the night, and then his brain caught up. His men were still out there.

He hoped so anyway.

Two more gunshots followed his ill-advised one. He heard a thud as a bullet struck the left side of the hull.

"Don't shoot at the chopper goddamnit!"

A chorus of howls greeted his shouted command. A scream was followed by three more gunshots.

Opening the door, the Colonel shoved the dead pilot out of the chopper and to the ground. Sliding into the chair, he closed the door. He'd flown years ago, but nothing this new. The controls still looked familiar. To the right of the joystick was mounted a Tremble GPS unit, and he set a waypoint so they could come back later for the body.

Or bodies, whatever the case might be.

With a flip of a switch, red landing lights lit up the clearing.

Three of his men stood back to back, facing outward. A pack of dogs surrounded them.

Not coyotes. Not wolves. Dogs. Most looked like mutts or even family pets gone crazy.

Eyes glowed yellow and orange. From medium to small, they faced inward. They sat in exactly the same position, as if commanded by some unseen presence to stay. Every time one of the soldiers raised his weapon a simultaneous growl rose from the pack as if from a single throat.

The men slowly edged their way to the chopper. When they got close, any dog blocking their way would stand and move warily around to the other side of the trio.

The pack allowed them to move, but not without caution.

They displayed amazing group intelligence, and a certain degree of domestication. There was no sign of the Sheriff or the fourth soldier.

Anderson wanted to start the motor but feared the unpredictable reaction of the dogs.

The first soldier reached the skid of the chopper and swung up inside as the two others swiveled their weapons outward to cover him, each careful not to raise the muzzle above waist level.

That seemed to be the line where the dogs considered them to be a threat.

After the first soldier made it inside, the other two others sat on the edge of the deck, sliding backwards and inside. As soon as their boots cleared the edge, they slid the door shut, and Colonel Anderson started the rotors turning. In the red-tinted light, he could see the dogs, arranged in six widening circles, staggered with military precision, facing inward, watching the chopper. A seventh circle of animals sat watching the woods.

"What about the Sheriff and Sergeant Jowan?" The soldiers shook their heads.

Anderson had no choice. He moved the collective, and the powerful turbines responded, lifting the machine from the forest floor and propelling it upward.

The rotors whipped at the dogs' fur of varying lengths and ears of varying floppiness and tossed them back and forth, but the animals remained still and watchful. *Something told them to stay*. The odd thought surfaced and once it did, he couldn't shake it.

He turned to head south, back to the Sheriff's office. He'd need to mount a ground search. A shiver went up his spine thinking of being chased by dogs again.

As the chopper rose, he saw the rows of dogs break up and race into the woods.

"What the hell was that?" One of the soldiers gave voice to his thoughts.

No one had an answer, and they rode in weighted silence through the night.

———

THE DRIVEWAY CAME UP FAST on the left, and I swung the Chevy in, but not too far. A chain blocked the way, but that wasn't the biggest problem.

I moved the chain to the right and clipped it into an eyelet on the post. An ornate spike decorated the top, and I carefully unscrewed it. Once the top rested in my hand, I reached inside the revealed cavity and flipped open a switch cover, changing the position from "on" to "off." Pulling the truck through the gap, I exited and reversed the procedure.

A camera faced the entrance, but no one would be watching. Not anymore. Everything looked the same as last time I left here.

Halfway down the drive, I stopped, getting out. Opening a crate in the back of the SUV, I removed a shovel and a pressure mine.

Moving the loose gravel aside, I assaulted the packed-down surface of the road. The first few inches didn't want to budge, but once I dug through that layer the work went faster.

Sparky exited the truck and sniffed the mine with mild interest. He turned and trotted off into the darkness. The moon remained hidden behind the horizon, and the darkness absorbed the dog's passage a few feet inside the perimeter of the trees. I wasn't worried.

Not about the dog.

A few moments later, the mine was buried. I smoothed the gravel over the plate and placed a forest service ribbon on one of the trees next to the road, marking its location. I probably didn't need the marker, but training was hard to ignore. By the time I was leaving, the bomb would already be detonated.

I moved to the east, setting a claymore and a trip wire on an old game trail. Game didn't use the trail anymore. No deer, elk, bear, or even cougar. They avoided this area like it was infected.

Because it was.

Another claymore set to the right, and I packed up the crate. One whistle and the dog came running.

"Good dog."

He wagged his tail as he leapt inside with normal canine enthusiasm.

We proceeded down the road, traveling nearly half a mile before we came to the abandoned guard shack. Razor wire topped the chain link fence in rusty loops all the way around the inner compound. Two buildings still stood. I looked to the right and saw the foundations jutting from the earth like the bottom half of a demon's jagged smile. They were all that remained of the building where they'd held me.

Looking away, I shuddered.

The building in the center of the compound, the place where *He* stayed would be my new residence.

Memories erupted in my head: shouts, screams of terror. I'd returned home, to where my troubles really began.

The stump of my finger itched fiercely, but I didn't touch it. Pulling the SUV next to the main building, I killed the engine.

I moved toward the guard shack at a brisk pace. Sparky again disappeared, this time down the fence line, nose to the ground in investigation, raising his leg on every fourth or fifth pole to mark his territory.

Once inside the guard shack, at the press of a green button, the rumble of a generator started under the ground.

Good. It still works. I could check the fuel situation later, but if the former occupants left even half a tank, I'd never drain it.

Pulling another lever caused a gate to rise from the ground, blocking the road I'd just driven in on.

A green light illuminated a button next to the lever, and I pressed it. A hum started, and a whole series of monitors came to life on the wall to my right. I pushed another button, and they shut down. I had no reason to waste the power since I would not be watching anyway.

There were twelve lights in two rows on the panel in front of me. All of them turned green except for one. Station nine. Its amber glow mocked me.

Not nine. Please.

I tapped the panel in what I knew was a vain gesture.

Time to go out for a closer look.

I exited the guard shack, not bothering to lock it. There was no reason to.

The perimeter security system, fully automated, armed, and nearly foolproof would alert me of anyone's approach. I knew because I'd designed it.

I whistled, but Sparky didn't come. I walked alone toward Station Nine, dreading what I'd find. My head throbbed as every fiber in my being told me not to go. Not to look. Not to awaken the memories.

It was too late. The time had come for me to face the past.

A TUGGING at the Sheriff's waist brought him back to consciousness. For a moment, he couldn't remember a thing.

Then he saw the body. The head hung from it at an odd angle, and a brown stain covered the front of its blouse like gravy spilled by an overindulgent child at Thanksgiving. But it wasn't gravy.

A dog furiously dug a hole thirty feet away, a weapon lying beside it.

The tugging stopped as his belt slid free. He moved to see what was going on, and another dog, this one sporting brown and black fur and Cocker-Spaniel-like ears growled deeply at him. He watched helplessly as a hound-like mutt dragged his gun and belt toward the industriously digging pup.

Two of what he figured for Doberman mixes stood in front of him, like guards.

Once the hound made its way a safe distance away, the brown and black cocker mix sat back on its haunches, watching closely. He stood, and none of the dogs moved to stop him. The trail leading to the chopper was only a few feet away. He stepped on to it, turning the way he'd come.

Brown and Black blocked his way. A low growl warned him.

He did an about face and started walking. The Shepherds took up positions on either side of the trail, and Brown and Black followed closely. He stopped, looking back.

The dog growled. He turned back to the trail again, and the dog barked, a single gunshot-like report.

He kept going. The dogs kept pace. A few minutes passed, and they came to the compound where they had been headed, and where their subject had been hiding.

A longtime resident of the area, he found it familiar. Few of these places existed that he hadn't visited from time to time to investigate gunshots or other strange activities. One building still smoldered. There were no signs of life.

The dogs let him stop, but not for long. With a growl, they let him know it was time to go and made no move to stop him when he moved to the driveway that led toward the main road. He assumed it was the way they wanted him to leave.

It took another ten minutes for them to reach the main road. The dogs stopped when he stepped out of the driveway. He took a few steps forward into the center of the road, and turned around.

The Dobermans sat side by side in the center of the driveway. Clearly, they weren't letting him go back that way.

Walking toward town, occasionally he glanced from side to side without spotting any dogs anywhere.

As he walked, he couldn't shake the feeling that he was being watched the whole time.

CHAPTER SIX

"Why would the FBI investigate the Army? Why wouldn't the Army investigate the Army?"

"Not the Army. An individual in the Army."

"Again, why not the Army?"

"We're more interested in what he is doing on his own time."

"Why me?"

"We can put you in a place you will be trusted."

"The Army knows and agrees to this?"

"Who do you think arranged all that in there? Do you really think they would separate a decorated soldier for something so mundane?"

"But—"

"No 'buts' Sergeant Clarke."

"I'm not—"

The agent handed him a military ID.

"Your name changed, and your pay just went up, too." He handed him a manila envelope. Clarke opened it. Inside were orders to Saudi Arabia. He was attached to a unit from Fort Bragg on special assignment from a 4th infantry division unit out of Fort Hood.

"Hood, really? You think they are going to buy this?"

"Yeah, they are. And you are going to sell it."

"Who are we watching?"

Rivas flipped a photo on to the table. "A certain Colonel Anderson."

He studied the photo, weighing his choices. An FBI rat in the Army or a ... what? He couldn't think of a single other thing he wanted to do.

"Do we have a deal? Or would you like to go back to being Sergeant Norwood?"

It only took a moment. He only knew how to do one thing. "I'll do it."

"Great." A smile crossed the agent's face, and he held out his hand. Norwood/Clarke shook it, hating the slimy feel. Somehow, he felt like he'd just made a deal with the devil.

———

SPARKY SAT ROOTED to the spot, and let out a whine as I came closer. I saw it.

There were bloodstains on the fence. They were mine. They'd persisted on the cold steel through at least one winter. The dog looked from left to right, growling.

He wanted to protect me, but he didn't know the threat was gone.

I spotted the problem with the security sensor. The wire right next to the post was cut. Hastily repaired with a wire nut and tape, the tape had disappeared, the wire nut lay a couple feet away. I grabbed the nut and knelt, twisting the wires back together.

I tried not to think, tried not to feel. It was a long time ago.

It felt like yesterday. It felt like years.

Run.

Run. Escape. Get out.

Get the fuck out! Hurry, hurry, before they see you here.

A shot rings out. I feel the slug strike my shoulder, and that's what gets me moving. I wriggle through the hole I've cut, my shoulder crying out at the effort. Parts of my flesh stay on the fence.

Don't care. Don't care. Run.

You can come back and kill them later.

Kill all these bastards for what they've done to you.

Bark!

Where did the fucking dog come from?

Bark! Bark!

I felt a shock and looked around.

My shoulder ached in sympathy at the memory, but there was no bullet. No wound.

No flesh on the fence. It had been repaired, if poorly. Just a blood stain. A blood stain from long ago.

A blood stain from yesterday.

Bark. Bark.

Okay, okay. I closed my eyes, trying to fight the voices, the memories in my head. I opened them and rose to my feet, steady again.

Sparky tugged at my sleeve, and I looked down. His eyes were filled with worry.

"It's okay, boy." Petting his head, I scratched his ears as we walked. His head was the perfect height and my hand rested lightly on top of it.

No doubt I'd have some time, but whoever came for me would be more prepared this time, so I needed to be, too.

There were only two answers to who might have been after me apart from bail bondsmen.

I didn't like either of them.

———

THE COLONEL PACED THE SIDEWALK. He stood in indecision at the edge of his power. Even as a colonel there was only so much he could do, so far he could push, so many orders he could give without a demand for an explanation coming from above his head.

A star on his lapel marked the next step in his career. Young enough to make those years count, he'd gain two things: more power, and a bigger retirement fund. Not that he didn't have a large one already, but most of that was funded by certain illicit acts he intended to keep secret.

The information at stake could cost him his military rank and his retirement if he wasn't sent to prison. The money ranked second to the Cause. If he didn't believe, if he hadn't recruited others that believed, it wouldn't matter.

It had taken time and effort to put together his unit, his team, to ensure they were all loyal. Lives had been lost. Clarke had always been a wild card.

Again, he wished he'd killed him when he'd had the chance. Who knew he'd get out, marry some rich bitch, and live so well off his goddamn disability? Who knew he'd stay enough in the game to preserve his connections?

Connections. Key number one in battle tactics. Cut off the enemy supply lines. He knocked three times on the huge oak door.

"Yes?" The door swung open to reveal a well-dressed servant.

"May I speak to Mrs. Clarke please?"

"She is indisposed. It's 6 a.m."

"Tell her it is Colonel Anderson. I have news of her husband."

"You'll have to make an appointment."

"I'm sure she'll see me..."

"Move aside, Zachary." The strong female voice came from the dark hall. "Show the Colonel to the sitting room. I'll be right there. Put some coffee on please."

For a family of wealth, the place was modest, but the sparse furnishings were of the highest quality: European, Germanic in character. The Colonel moved in, finding a seat, and did something the Army had taught him to do well: he waited.

Ten minutes passed, and then fifteen. The smell of coffee invaded the room first, followed by the smell of bacon. His stomach growled, and in spite of his growing impatience he recognized a growing hunger. He hadn't eaten in hours, and the little sleep he'd caught on the ride over left his body wanting.

A tall blonde walked in. Not at all what he'd expected, her bare legs led up to a short silk robe fastened loosely at the waist. Her long neck descended into visible cleavage. Startling green eyes appraised him as he looked her over.

"Join me for breakfast? I'm afraid I'm rather hungry, and didn't sleep much."

"Me either, thanks to your husband..."

She turned and he saw a fire light inside her eyes. "Do you think that my lack of sleep is for some other reason?"

"No ma'am."

"I've invited you to join me for two reasons, Colonel. One is to discuss my husband and his whereabouts now. The second is to discuss how to get him out of this. Specifically, how much it will cost."

"Ma'am, it's not a matter of cost so much as—"

A second later her face was inches from his. Her chest was pressed tightly against his arm and he could smell sweet mint on her breath as she spoke. "Colonel, my husband and I have discussed you before, and he said you were a man that could be bought for the right price. Was he wrong?"

Her finger reached up and traced the outline of his eyes, walked down the foothills of his face, and her hand cupped his chin. He could look nowhere else but her eyes, and realized he'd been holding his breath. He let it out in a whoosh of air, and she backed away.

"Should we discuss this over breakfast, or should I bid you good day?"

A mistake. Coming here had been a mistake. He couldn't walk away now though, could he? His stomach growled, and he opened his mouth, but before he could answer, she laughed.

"Your stomach just answered for you. Come, Colonel. Talking never hurt, did it?" The twirl she executed before leading him toward an as yet unseen dining room revealed that little or nothing covered her body under the silk robe.

Aroused, sick, and hungry all at the same time, he followed her anyway, no longer in control.

———

THE SOUNDS of night had turned to the sounds of morning before anyone came along. Occasionally he heard a howl or a bark, evidence that the dogs were still around, watching, but he didn't see any. Headlights lit the road, followed by the rattle of a motor in need of a tune up, and he stepped off the edge of the road to flag the driver down.

"Ted?"

"Hi Wayne."

"What you doin' walking out here?"

"Long story. Can you get me back into Riggins? Better yet Grangeville?"

"Yeah, I'm headed that way. What happened?"

"I'll tell ya' while we drive."

"Well hop in. I gotta get feed and get it back before Leslie thinks I stopped somewhere for breakfast."

"And missed out on her pancakes? She'd never believe it."

Sheriff Crawford jumped in, slamming the door on the old Ford.

"Not a word to the missus about what I'm going to tell you. Last thing we need around here is a panic."

"You got my word. I won't tell a soul."

"Maybe you can help me out later if I need it."

"Sure. Anything for ya'."

———

TRAPS SET. Security set. Nothing remained but waiting.

Waiting is a soldier's game. Something I'd been taught well in the fields of Afghanistan and the desert of Saudi Arabia. Most of your time is spent waiting for something to happen, and when it does, you wish you were bored all over again.

The top floor of the headquarters building afforded a three-hundred-and-sixty-degree view of the entire compound. Video monitors dominated one corner, showing no less than 18 cameras covering the perimeter. Paranoia played into my hands.

Air conditioning hummed, keeping the temperature bearable. The Lieutenant had insisted on it when I designed this room. I dozed in the chair that once belonged to him. An alarm would sound at any movement, any approach.

Sparky lay at my feet, exhausted. I found some dog food, stale, but clearly edible by his reaction. A bowl of water sat nearby. Belly full, he rested, content.

He seemed to want to be near me. If I left the room, he followed, even if I went down the hall to take a piss. He remained alert, head picking up at every sound.

I looked with longing at the phone on the desk. I knew the line was secure and untraceable. I'd set it up.

Marsha, on the other hand, would be talking on our home phone or her cell. Both were probably bugged by now. Maybe I'd make a quick call later, just to let her know I was okay.

Sleep pulled my eyelids closed like there were weights hanging from them. I couldn't keep them open. I drifted and dreamed, the warrior silent for now.

———

"MRS. CLARKE."

"Call me Marsha. Cream? Sugar?"

"No thanks. Listen, your husband's situation—"

"He jumped bail. You want a reward for bringing him back? I've already made a deal with the prosecuting attorney's office."

"You have? What might that be?"

"Lenience, in exchange for information."

"What kind of information?"

"Oh, my husband knows all kinds of things. And I have a private investigator looking into the so-called accident, and the shooting that followed. I don't think everything is what it appears."

"Some kind of conspiracy?" He sneered openly. "How exactly did that work?"

"I'm not sure, Colonel."

"Call me Mike, if I'm going to call you Marsha."

"No thanks, Colonel." She folded her arms. "Well?"

"Well what, ma'am?"

"What's really going on?"

"Ma'am—"

"Marsha."

"Okay, Marsha. I'm not sure I know what you mean. Your husband killed a man. Jumped bail that you posted. I came here to ask you questions, not the other way around."

"So Colonel, why is the Army interested in the fact that my husband, now a civilian, jumped bail on a local murder charge that seems suspicious at best. It was self-defense, right?"

"I don't know the details."

"I want to know why you're here then."

"Because with your husband's skills and training, the FBI asked for our help. Since I've served with him, they think I may be able to help."

"Really?"

"Yes."

"So they know you're here?"

"Perhaps not specifically, but they know of my involvement."

A smile toyed at the corner of her lips. She took a bite of scrambled egg, chewing daintily.

He picked up a slice of bacon, and bit off the end.

"You're lying." She made the statement after swallowing her egg.

"I assure you, I'm not."

"But you are. The FBI was here last night. The ATF. Every

three-letter agency in the book. The locals have enlisted help, because they think my husband left the country because of his ties, or he plans to. They're watching me to see if I give away where he goes. Yet here you are. Someone he served with, not even asking yet where he is. I think you know better than I do where he might be. I think you want to scare me into cutting him off, financially and otherwise, and enlist my help in getting him to surrender. Is that about right?"

"Mrs. Clarke, if he would just turn himself in, we could end all this."

"All what? I haven't heard from Todd since he left. He took cash, lots of it. No, I don't know how much. Yes, I know he has connections, and could leave the country. He won't. He wants to clear his name. He turned me on to the smell of something fishy and told me something else."

"What's that?"

"He told me you showing up would confirm his suspicions, and not to tell you anything."

"So why did you invite me in?"

"He asked me to give you something."

"Really? What might that be?"

She slapped him hard, and he fell to the floor. Her bare foot kicked out, bruising the side of his face. He blocked the next kick, but a flash of silk distracted him. He rose to his knees, struggling to stand.

"I'll have you arrested!"

"No, you won't. He said to tell you I have a letter."

"A letter."

"Yeah, here's your copy. He wants to know what's really happening. I don't think he expected this manhunt, but you can call it off too. That's my demand."

"If I don't?"

"You know the deal, Colonel. In 48 hours, I either destroy the letter I have, and instruct the others with copies to do the same, or if anything happens to me or Todd, or if they don't get a call from me saying otherwise, they go in the mail. Your envelope is addressed too."

He studied the address: *General Malden, Pentagon. Department of Homeland Security.* He looked up at her, sudden hate in his eyes. "I'll kill him."

"We're on the same side now. Kill him, kill your career."

He stood speechless. "Anything else?" he managed.

"One more thing." She dropped the robe to the floor. Underneath she wore nothing but a black thong. Staring helplessly, his chin dropped to his chest as she took two steps forward.

Her foot moved swiftly, and pain exploded in his crotch. Doubling over, he struggled for air.

"That one is from me. For ogling me the whole time you've been here. Todd taught me how to fight too. Now get out. Don't come back until he's in the clear."

It couldn't be true. He picked himself up, angry, in pain, and struggled out the door. The sunlight stabbed holes into his eyes, and he pulled out his sunglasses. Broken.

Bitch broke his sunglasses! Hate wasn't a strong enough word.

He strode to his car. His driver stared but looked quickly away as he dropped into the back seat.

"Home," he said without preamble.

He threw the broken shades to the floor and tore open the envelope. His face stiffened as he read. There were internet links too. He typed them in to his tablet. Password protected files he couldn't delete. Photos. Videos of meetings.

Clarke was a fucking rat. It wasn't safe to exterminate him until he cleared up this mess. And what about the fucking dogs last night? What was that about?

He closed his eyes. A few winks on the way to the hotel, and then what? He'd come up with something. He always did.

CHAPTER SEVEN

The light bulb swung back and forth, bare and hypnotic. "Why are you here?"

He wanted so much to just answer, but timing was everything. Icy water poured over his head from above, and he gasped as it rolled over his chin, into his mouth. Breathing became a struggle.

"You're FBI?"

As he'd been trained, he gave no answer.

"You will talk to me. I assure you. Why not make this easier for both of us?"

Nothing.

"Fine then." The interrogator nodded to someone standing outside his field of vision.

Excruciating pain raced through his spine, and he tilted his head back, trying to escape it. As he did, the water dumped over his head again. He gulped, swallowed, and breathed water into his lungs.

He coughed, wanting to bend forward and expel the liquid, but the spasm in his back made it impossible. Water fountained from his mouth, and he tried to exhale, tried not to take any more in, but with every effort more entered his lungs.

He would drown soon, and death would be welcome. He wouldn't die *a hero: that he was sure of. The number of people who knew he was here was less than the remaining whole fingers on his left hand.*

Escape was his only option, and at the moment he wouldn't allow himself hope. Death seemed much more likely.

The light of the room became a pinpoint at the end of a dark tunnel, and he felt himself slipping away from reality.

This is it. This is the end.

Just then the pain in his back stopped, and his retreat to unconsciousness quickly reversed itself as a coughing fit took over. He doubled over as far as his restraints would allow and sent what felt like a gallon of water shooting on to the dust-covered concrete.

Someone grabbed his hair, pulling his neck backwards. His eyes met those of his questioner.

"You will talk, or you will die slowly. Stop torturing yourself."

The hand let his hair go, and his head fell back between his knees. He heard a shuffling as the two men left the room. Just before the door clanged shut, he heard the second voice speak for the first time since entering the room.

"Sweet dreams, my friend."

Not responding, he promised himself not to forget that voice and felt a sudden determination to live.

Or at least to try.

————

THE BURNER PHONE RANG.

"Ditch the phone." The caller disconnected.

It wasn't a question. I dropped the phone into a sink in the corner and ran water over it, until the screen went black, shut off the water, took the battery out, and set it on the mahogany desk. I put the remains of the phone in my back pocket.

I checked all the monitors. Still nothing. Good. Bad.

The buzzing of the warrior began. My instincts tingled. The electricity of battle electrified the air. Wilson didn't do anything without a reason.

"C'mon Sparky," I called.

He rose, padding along beside me. I scratched his head, and the buzzing quietened to a dull vibration. He calmed me.

Making my way to the shed out back, I placed the phone on a bench and pulverized it with a hammer.

The SUV sat against the building where I'd parked it. Opening the back, I retrieved a second burner hidden under the spare tire.

I turned it on.

A beep sounded once it booted up.

A text message waited. "Anderson's gone fishing."

At least I now knew who I was dealing with. Time to call Marsha and see if she'd delivered the package yet.

Not from the new phone. Not yet. I headed back upstairs, stopping briefly in the kitchen. From the pantry, I grabbed an MRE. It'd do for now.

I grabbed a cup of the stale dog food too, and Sparky barked his approval. Lunch time. Maybe our last sane meal for a while.

———

"TODD!" she squealed. "Are you okay?"

"For now. Can't talk long, just in case. Did you deliver the package?"

"He stopped by for it this morning. You were right."

"Any other clues yet?"

"None. Baby, when can you come home?"

"I'll let you know. Honey?"

"Yeah?"

"I love you. Keep up the dumb blonde act, okay? It will be okay soon."

"I kicked him in the nuts."

"You what?"

"I kicked him in the nuts before he left. I couldn't help myself."

"I'm sure he deserved it. I don't deserve you. You're amazing. I hate putting you through this."

"Be safe."

"Love you."

"You too."

The call ended.

"Did you get all that?" the agent asked.

"Yeah."

"A trace?"

"Impossible. It kept jumping around. Except ..."

"Except what?"

"It's not international. I'd bet it's regional, because of the way the signal worked. No delay either."

"Regional?"

"Somewhere in the Northwest. Give me more time with him on the line, more time to set up equipment, I'll get you a better fix."

"Okay. Okay. Who do we have on the Colonel?"

"Team C. Best we could do."

"Tell them to be discreet, but to get taps into place as soon as possible."

"Yes, Sir."

The FBI was getting better. No one would have spotted the surveillance truck. It was housed in a Dodge Caravan with a family silhouette bumper sticker, and a little "dachshund on board" triangle. A lei hung from the rearview mirror. More crowded, at least it didn't scream surveillance.

"Why are they so interested in this Clarke guy anyway? I know he jumped bail, they say he killed a cop, but come on."

"You don't need to know, so stop asking."

"Just curious."

"Well, curiosity killed the cat." The lead agent chastised the junior agent, but added a thought of his own, silently.

Satisfaction brought him back. His orders to observe and report came from the highest levels.

Outside the van, the camera showed a dog that stopped and took a piss on the tire. It sniffed at the sliding door and moved on.

———

THE BELL DINGED over the door, and Dale Fischer grumbled audibly. He'd spent until 1 a.m. chasing some dead-beat dad down hiding up on the lake with a boat he'd bought with the alimony he owed his ex-wife in Texas. True, it sounded like she was a bitch too, but she paid well: twenty percent for recovery. Since he was $40,000 behind, and the boat itself was worth at least that, his cut was eight grand. Not bad for what turned out to be about 8 hours' work. Sure, the guy would be pissed when he woke up and found the boat gone, but then that's why Dale never married. Girlfriends? Sure, he'd even live with them if they wanted, but his job taught him one thing: marriage almost always turned out to be a bad deal for both parties.

Chasing bail fugitives was almost always a night game, so he wasn't used to functioning well before noon. Today, even noon felt early.

"You Dale Fischer?" The questioner was short, wore a hooded sweatshirt, and seemed more like someone he'd chase rather than a client. He carried a dirty duffel bag he set down at his feet.

"Depends who's asking. What can I do for you?"

"I want you to fetch a fugitive for me."

"Okay. Who and for what?"

"Jumped bail on a murder rap."

"Who?" He kept up on the local cases, and figured this one must be from out of state.

"Todd Clarke."

"Marsha Clarke's husband? The cop killer? There's already guys on that, better than me. They figure he ran out of the country."

"I have information that says he's hiding locally."

"Share it with the FBI then. Local cops. That one's out of my league."

Truth be told, he didn't want to enter the fray. There was interest on all sides, and reportedly big money. The kind of money that bounty hunters shot each other over to get to the client, who then might shoot them. It just wasn't his thing.

"An interested party wants you on this one."

"I don't know any of the interested parties."

"This might help." He unzipped the duffel. Inside, Dale saw stacks of twenty-dollar bills.

He shook his head. "I still don't think so."

"Fischer, this is just up-front payment. Call it expense money. The interested party would like Mr. Clarke brought quietly to him, not necessarily to the authorities, if you know what I mean."

"I do, and I got out of that a long time ago. I'm strictly legit now."

"A certain Colonel would like you to call on some of your Brotherhood you may still be in contact with. He says they have a personal interest in Clarke, and so do you."

"Look, whoever you are, I'm not interested."

The stranger tossed an envelope on the counter. "Look that over. Keep the money, for now. If after you do your research, you still want out, I'll come back for it then."

"Listen, I already told you I'm not interested."

The stranger turned and walked out the door, the bell ringing with finality. Dale fingered the envelope, and then slid it open.

On top were four 8 x 10 prints, black and white, but clear shots.

The man in them looked so much younger. A life he'd put behind him. A scar on his bicep was all that remained of the swastika tattoo he'd had removed last year.

The shovel in his hands, the white sheet folded up onto the top of his head. The gallows.

The grave behind him. The Lieutenant's arm around his shoulder.

The camp sign in the next picture. Todd Clarke in the background, watching. He picked up the phone, then thought better of it. Pay phones had become nearly impossible to find. Time to go buy a pre-paid cell and make some calls.

This would be the last time, no matter what. Of course, that's what he'd said the last time.

———

Darkness brought with it the time for wakefulness. Soldiers ruled the night. I did.

The cameras switched to infrared as the light faded, with the aid of a light sensor built in. Solar panels powered them, reducing the load on the generator and the need to run wires. A brilliant stroke, even if I said so myself.

I saw movement, and then warm bodies. First on camera one, and then on camera eighteen. Then two. Seventeen. Three. Sixteen. An alarm sounded, but I silenced it. I was already watching. The forms weren't human.

Sparky wasn't at my feet anymore, and the door was ajar. I glanced at the cameras again. There were two canine-like forms visible in every screen.

"What the hell?" There was no danger tingling, no rising of the warrior. I stared, and then I saw new movement in one of the monitors. A canine figure moved inside the fence.

Sparky.

He disappeared from one camera and appeared in another. I watched in fascination as for twenty minutes, he made a circuit of the compound. Once he passed their position, the dogs didn't move. The forms appeared to be on guard.

Needing to see for myself, I rushed down the stairs two at a time. I approached the gate. On the road, at the edge of my vision, sat two mutts. Doberman mixes by the look, side by side, facing away from me. I walked the perimeter.

Sometimes I saw them. Other times I didn't, but I could guess their positions. Besides, I didn't need to see them. I felt them. Sparky trotted along beside me, quietly panting. I completed the circuit and headed back up the stairs. He followed. Once we entered the security room, he looked up at me.

Did I do good? His eyes asked.

"Good boy," I said, but not too loud, not knowing why, just feeling the urge to keep quiet. "Thanks."

He went over to the wall of monitors, watching. I didn't know dogs could process TV images, but he seemed to both see and understand.

Sipping water, I watched, knowing all too well that nothing at all might happen tonight.

I had the Colonel on his heels. At least, I hoped so.

———

"Come on in."

"I thought you were out."

"Me too."

"Who this time?"

"Todd Clarke."

"I thought we were through with him."

"So did I. But I have this report. And a map."

"What's this?"

"His last location, and the direction he headed."

"So if we draw a circle here..."

"Yeah."

"Holy shit. You know where he is."

"Probably is."

"Dale, this is huge. We could turn him in. The reward..."

"No. We get him, we call this number, they pick him up."

"Really?" He took a moment to look at the number.

"How much?"

"A thousand a man, just to show up tonight. Double that if we get him."

"How many men do you want?"

"A dozen at least."

"I don't know if I can get that many."

"Time on target, 4 a.m. This may turn into a recon, and recock tomorrow. If it is, they still get paid, both nights."

"Still."

"Cash up front. Meet here at 1 a.m."

"I'll do my best."

"Do better. I want to be done with this."

As the man left, Dale turned the sign to 'Closed' and locked the door. He needed some things out of storage before everyone showed up.

"Ricky, come."

His big Lab mix stretched and padded close behind him as he headed out the back door.

"He took it."

"Yeah." The solider stripped off his hoodie and grinned.

"Untraceable to me?"

"Completely."

"The other matter?"

"We'll handle it."

"You're sure?"

"Yes, Sir."

"I'm counting on you."

"Sir, when have we ever let you down?"

"Only once."

The soldier's expression hardened. "It won't happen again Colonel."

"Good."

Anderson walked out, intending to go to bed early. By morning, hopefully this would all be over.

———

"What is all this, Sherrie?"

"Stuff I wouldn't normally put on your desk, but it seems really odd."

"Give it to me in a nutshell. I'm a bit pressed for time."

"They're all reports of missing dogs."

"Missing dogs?"

"Yeah, missing dogs. Dogs that have either mysteriously run away or gone missing in the last 72 hours."

"How many dogs are we talking about here?"

"Dozens."

"All from our area?"

"Pretty much."

All the dogs last night. Mutts mostly. He glanced through the list, trying to let his mind make sense of it on its own.

"Who's on this?"

"James has been out to interview some of the owners, but it's all in the reports. The dogs disappeared. No trace, no blood, sign of foul play. Just dogs that have been faithful, some for years, and suddenly got a wild hair and ran off."

He knew how it was. Rural area. Half the damn things were never fenced or chained up. They had free reign. One or two, he would've mounted a search for a cougar or bobcat come to hunt. But this list? And last night?

He had no idea what to think.

"Let me know if he turns up anything on this. I'm going home to shower before anything else happens."

"Yes, Sir. I'll keep in touch. What happened with the Army guys last night?"

"Don't know. We got separated. Even if that goddamn colonel calls, tell him he can wait."

"You got it, but no one has called all day. Except about the dogs."

He shook his head. The military comes in. Uses him for his knowledge. Even asks for his men to help. And then they disappear?

Typical feds. Fuck 'em, he needed some rest.

Heading out he noted even the usual strays weren't digging in the trash in the park. Weird.

CHAPTER EIGHT

"*A*re you ready to talk?"

He feigned more weakness than he felt. He had no idea if he had the strength to do what he needed to, but if he died trying?

C'est la vie.

Or c'est la mort.

He let his head roll back and forth on his shoulders as the interrogator dragged the chair forward.

He felt the back of a hand strike the side of his face.

He began to twitch, flopping his limbs rapidly against the bonds, and let his tongue rest against the back of his throat, causing him to gag.

"Cut him loose!" He heard the order. It started as a fake seizure, but his weakened body gave in, and he felt himself starving for oxygen, coughing more than he wanted to, his vision dimming.

He fought the weakness, the unconsciousness. Closed his eyes and waited.

Sensed a face close to his. Felt a finger press itself against his neck, checking for a pulse. Heard the throbbing of his heart in his ears.

Fast.

Too fast. One shot.

He threw his eyes open, brought his arms up, grabbed the back of the interrogator's neck, and bit down on his nose as hard as he could.

Aggghhhhh!!!

His arms couldn't hold for long, but he tightened his jaw. The flesh of the man's nose tore as he pulled away, and he gagged on the blood and snot that flowed down his throat. He turned on his side and coughed violently, seeing the laced boots of the assistant, the owner of the accented voice.

The time was now or never. He grabbed the boot while the man was distracted, and with all of his meager strength twisted. The man fell, the crunch of bone striking the concrete snapped like a gunshot through the still air, audible over the screams of the bitten man.

No time for satisfaction. Look around for a weapon. Anything.

Bolt cutters, lying on the bench. He pushed himself to his knees, staggered to his feet. The interrogator rolled in helpless agony on the floor, blood streaming from his face, running like a spring-swollen stream between his fingers. His assistant lay still but let out a moan as he risked a look.

Grabbing the bolt cutters and flexing them open, he revealed the sharp inner edges. Who knew what torture they'd been intended for, but he had other ideas. He stepped in and swung, first at the head of the moaning assistant. One blow silenced him. Spreading the jaws of the cutters as far as he can, he pinched the fold of skin at the side of the unconscious neck, where he could see the pulse throbbing the vein. Brought the handles together.

The resulting fountain of blood surprised him, even though he'd expected something. He darted out of the way, but still not managing to avoid getting soaked. He nearly stumbled over the now-gasping interrogator. "Yoooff fuggghh!" The man's mangled nose defied his ability to form coherent speech, but his hands managed a weak grip on Clarke's knees. Shaky already, the tiny interference toppled him. The disfigured apparition began to crawl up his body. He wanted to torture this man as he'd been tortured. Wanted to take his time, mess him up. A warning in the back of his head tells him he has no time for that. It's kill or be killed.

Bringing the bolt cutters around, he managed a hit to the shoulder that only slowed his assailant. Muscles shaking, he swung them around one more time. His left hand slipped free and the momentum opens the jaws of the cutters wide.

The injured interrogator turned at the last moment, and the right blade entered his eye socket and sticks there. He screamed, the sound filling Clarke's world.

Grasping at one final opportunity, he felt his grip loosening as the man struggled, but he managed to get his left hand back on the handle while retaining his grip on the righ, and closed the jaws.

It sounded like a twig breaking when the cutters severed the cartilage that made up the bridge of the man's nose. His eyes now had no home, their sockets shattered. Blood fountained over Clarke for the second time. Struggling out from under the body, he felt the need to run; surely there must be others.

Surely they heard the screaming and the commotion.

Surely they must be on their way.

Flee or die.

As he struggled, the bolt cutters swung back and forth in his right hand. With one last tug, he pulled his legs free, but with that effort the cutters slipped, swinging in an unfortunate arc, striking him square in the forehead. He felt consciousness speed away, and as it did, he heard ironic maniacal laughter echo inside his head.

———

"You're sure?"

"It's the only place he can be. And the generator's running."

"What if it's not him?"

"What do you mean?"

"What if it's somebody else in there?"

"Like who?"

"The fucking Lieutenant come back, or some such? How the fuck would I know?"

"Okay, I got an idea."

"What's that, Fischer?"

"You march up, knock on the fucking door, and ask who's home."

"It beats your idea of breaking in."

"Okay look, see that Chevy over there?"

Jasper dropped his reading glasses to his chest and put the binoculars to his eyes. "Yeah, I see it."

"It fits the description of what he was drivin'."

"There's a million of those things around."

"Who knows about this place?"

"Plenty of people."

"Who knows how to turn on the gen sets?"

"A few less people."

"Now look over there."

Jasper swung the binoculars to follow his finger. "Gates up. What about it?"

"Who knows how to raise the fucking gate?"

"Okay, so it's probably him. What's the plan?"

"Gather your men, and I'll tell you. If he's armed the security system, and I'm sure he has, and if he's watching, which I'm sure he is, getting close unseen is going to be hard."

"But you know how."

"I know how." He pulled a pack with two antennas sticking out of the top from the back of his truck.

"What's that?"

"This, my friend, is how."

As he shut the tailgate, Ricky whimpered in the passenger seat. "No, you can't come, boy. Stay."

Ricky growled, deep in his throat, looking into the night.

"Shut up dog. Stay."

Ricky growled again, but quietly, and stayed, just as he was told.

———

With a violent jerk of my limbs I was awake. Sparky barked and tugged at my sleeve.

I glanced at the monitors, rotating my head to free the crick threatening to immobilize my neck. Nothing. Just dogs sitting.

Wait.

Not sitting.

Their profiles had changed.

They were lying down. Making themselves harder to see. Not from my side, but from the other side.

I glanced at the clock. 4:30. Perfect time for an assault. I should've set an alarm by it. As I watched, camera one wavered, the colors mixing into squiggly lines, finally surrendering to meaningless static.

"Good dog. You woke me up just in time."

Sparky wagged his tail, but remained quiet, watching me as if evaluating what I might do next.

I picked up my night vision goggles and headed out to the balcony, taking a rifle with a bi-pod hanging from the barrel. The .300 caliber rounds and a night vision scope should allow me to reach out and touch at least the first of my visitors.

I set up quietly, resting my elbows on the balcony ledge, the glasses against my eyes. Straight ahead of the gate, I saw human shapes moving.

They moved in a loose 'V' formation, but they committed the communal sin all amateur troops do: they stayed too close together. If I was an enemy with a grenade...

Then I remembered the claymores and the pressure IED I'd placed on the way in. I checked their position again.

Thirty more feet. I considered. Did I want to waste my good tricks on amateurs? Their knowledge of my position compromised this fortress, but it was one of the most defensible in the area. Given another 24 hours to rest and resurrect old contacts...

The decision made itself as they moved closer.

Fuck it. Let 'em have it. A better unit would've spotted the traps and avoided them. A quick count revealed an even dozen.

One in the center of the road, dumbass. Two others would likely trip the claymores. If not, I had enough rounds to take care of them. Swinging the rifle to the ready, I looked around. Sparky had disappeared again.

Then I heard the first bark, and knew some decisions were out of my hands.

———

"SPREAD OUT." Dale sent the command for the third time. Community syndrome ran deep with these fucking amateurs. You're not safer next to your buddy. Not when your enemy consisted of good soldiers.

Correction, a good soldier. It was just one guy, although Clarke had a hell of a reputation.

"Jasper, get off the road," he whispered into his mike. *What the hell was that guy thinking?*

He watched as Jasper slowly started to sidestep, and then he heard a bark from his far right. A scream immediately followed the sound, and then Jasper opened fire.

"Over here!" He yelled. "Guard dogs." He took three steps forward, and the stillness shattered into a million pieces as a ball of flame rose from where he'd been standing a moment before.

He didn't die right away. Instead he screamed.

When his eyes adjusted to the sudden brightness, Dale looked to the road, and saw half a man sitting there.

"Help! Help!"

Dale knew there was only one way to help Jasper now. Put him down like a dog with a festering broken leg.

He brought his rifle around to do just that, but before he could, Jasper's head exploded. Clarke was there after all, and watching.

Time slowed. Just as he realized what was really going on, another scream came, this time from his left, followed by growling and a burst of gunfire. The growling continued and the scream stopped. Then, as darkness once again descended, the night filled with snarls, barks, and growls.

Dale did the only logical thing. He ran back the way they'd come.

———

THE WARRIOR QUIETED QUICKLY.

What a mess!

No real targets appeared after the first injured man. Dog and human forms met and rolled to the ground. The forms remained still, the dogs moved on.

One figure ran back down the road, I assumed the way the men had come. A canine form chased it.

Kill. The warrior whispered.

I took aim on the form for a second.

Save the ammo. Let the dog take care of him. Sparky stared at me, and I knew the voice was his.

I lowered the rifle and heard the sound of a dog lapping water from a bowl. Sparky was quenching his thirst.

"Good work," I told him.

Sparky looked up and wagged his tail happily. "Do your friends need anything? Food? Water?" Two barks, then a shake of his head.

"No?"

He ran and chased his tail, then bounded from one end of the room to the other. Victory made him a playful puppy.

I laughed and chased him. He grabbed at the air, growled, barked, and danced, panting the whole time.

I wished I had a ball to throw for him.

I wished I'd grown up with a dog like Sparky. Emotion overwhelmed me, and I sat down in the chair, tears streaming down my face, head in my hands.

Sparky stopped his prancing and came to me. I felt his nose, pressing, prying my hands apart. He licked the tears from my eyes.

I'd never felt such love for a creature before. I threw my arms around him and dried my tears on his smooth fur. He stood, supporting me, letting me release my emotions, until the sobs dried up, and I straightened in the chair. In front of any being other than Marsha, I would've felt embarrassment and shame. In front of Sparky, I felt only love and acceptance.

His tail wagged once, twice. *Are you okay?* he asked.

I nodded and he barked, tail wagging harder.

For the first time in a long time, I felt sane.

———

DALE RAN. He heard the dog behind him, panting, gaining fast.

Just ahead he saw the clearing. Air raced in and out of his lungs, scorching their insides along the way. One more burst of speed. He couldn't tell if the hot breath on the back of his neck was real or imagined.

A root reached out and grabbed his ankle, pulling him to the ground.

Oh, no. Fuck no.

He heard a growl, followed by another from the direction he was running. The breeze of something flying over him brushed his cheek, and he rolled to his feet.

Behind him, he saw a gray and white patched mongrel wrestling on the ground with a big black Lab.

"Ricky! Come here, boy."

The dog didn't heed his command, as both animals fought in a ball of tangling, biting fur, growling and scratching at each other, each seeking purchase to gain its feet, looking for an opening to best the other. Ricky landed on his paws, and jumped forward, biting his attacker on the flank. Blood and fur mixed as the dog yelped, and turned to stare down the Lab.

Ricky barked, and the mutt flinched.

"Good boy," Dale slowly raised his rifle, looking for a clean shot. "Ricky, move," he commanded.

The dogs stood stock still, their gazes locked. Both panted.

Ricky barked again. The mutt broke eye contact and looked down at the ground. The Lab strode forward, standing over the bent head of his subdued foe.

The mutt whined, a melodic speech-like whine. Ricky's ears perked up, then he cocked his head, whining back. They went back and forth a couple more times, as if having a conversation.

Dale watched with interest. Ricky had never acted that way.

"Ricky come!"

Ricky bowed his head to the other dog, and the mutt turned and scampered into the woods. The other dog came slowly back to the truck, seeming almost reluctant to return.

Dale yanked open the passenger door. The window that he'd let down only a few inches was now open almost all the way. On the old-fashioned crank handle, he saw fresh teeth marks.

He turned, and the big Lab jumped humbly in, immediately lying on the seat, tapping his tail.

Don't be mad, the look said. Dale knew the look from when Ricky was a puppy stealing shoes and socks, absconding with them to the back yard. He patted the dog on the head, but rolled up the window, leaving just a crack, before shutting the door again.

"Good dog. I'm not mad." *How could he be?* Ricky had likely saved his life.

But he'd never done anything like that before. As Dale climbed into the truck and started the engine, he looked around at the chaos and realized he was the only one leaving out of the dozen men who'd arrived with him. He shuddered, wondering what would have happened if his dog hadn't interfered.

As Dale shifted the truck into gear, Ricky whined and looked back the way they'd come with longing in his eyes, as if leaving behind a favorite toy.

CHAPTER NINE

No one came.

He had no idea how long he'd been out.

Blood decorated the floor. His captors were dead, and he took quick inventory of his wounds.

He was hurt and weak, but able to move. Had to move.

He struggled to his feet and grabbed the bolt cutters as he rose. They were the only weapon handy, and he felt better carrying something.

The door swung open easily. His assailants hadn't locked it behind them. He looked right and left. All quiet. Eventually someone would conclude that it was too quiet and come to investigate.

The fence was only ten yards away, but it felt like a mile with no cover. He rubbed his forearm over his eyes to clear his vision and ambled forward, managing to keep his feet. He dropped to his knees by the fence and cut the wire first that he knew would trigger the alarm. After all, he'd set up the security system, so knew how to disable it.

If they were watching the cameras, they would see him.

He cut through the fence with the cutters from the bottom. He worked as quickly as he could, a link at a time. A foot and a half.

Two feet. It would have to be enough.

He rolled on his back and started to wriggle underneath. "There he is!"

The shout was distant, and he wriggled faster. "Shoot him you fool! He's escaping!"

The shot rang out.

The bullet entered his shoulder, exited the back. Excruciating pain followed. He pushed through anyway.

Stumbled to his feet. Dropped the bolt cutters.

Heard another bullet whine off the gravel near his feet. Stumbled, struggled into a staggering trot toward where he knew there was a road.

Staggered for minutes on end. Hours.

Days.

Weeks. He had no idea.

He stumbled on to the road. His world filled with light. The scratch of tires on gravel. A voice.

"What the hell?"

"Get him in the back."

"Get on the CB. Let them know we're coming in." Darkness. Waking.

Red and blue lights. A hospital? Fade out. Fade in.

A chopper. Flying.

Darkness. Darkness. Darkness.

———

"You're telling me there are eleven men dead or missing, killed by what?"

"Dogs."

"A pack of dogs?"

"Yes."

"You expect me to believe that?"

"If Ricky here hadn't jumped in and saved me, it'd be twelve dead or missing." Dale patted the Lab and scratched between his ears. The dog shook his head. He seemed restless.

"So now Clarke has a pack of wild dogs protecting his compound, and they chased off or killed a dozen armed men?"

"We weren't expecting them, Sir. No one told us a thing about the dogs, or we could have done better."

"You'll go in again."

"All due respect, Colonel, no I won't. I'm a hired hand, and I don't get paid enough to risk my life and those of any more of my friends."

"Then get the fuck out of here!"

Ricky growled at the outburst.

"Easy boy," Dale soothed.

"That's right. Control your dog before he comes at me like the ones that bested you."

"We'll be going now. Best of luck, Colonel." Ricky followed him out the door. The Colonel turned to the soldier.

"They still can't trace this back to me, right?"

"Affirmative, Sir."

"Get in touch with some kind of animal control, and get them out there to round up those fucking dogs."

"That's not a good idea, Sir."

"Why not?"

"The local Sheriff is already looking into them."

"What? Who tipped him off?"

"A bunch of local dogs have disappeared. One or two might have been accepted as coyotes or cougars, or even runaways. But there have been dozens."

"Dozens?"

"Yes, Sir."

"How is this connected to Clarke?"

"We have no idea, Sir. He wasn't even a K-9 in the military. No history with dogs that we know of, and I know his file well."

"So he has an accomplice that ... what? Is a Pied Piper for dogs?"

"We haven't gotten close enough to tell."

"So get close enough. Get a drone to do a flyover with thermal imaging. Get me some intel, dammit!"

"Sir, it is getting harder and harder..."

"There are some drones at Mountain Home. Tell those Air Force pukes it's a Priority One training objective. Tell them to fly them in from as far away as they can without having to consult Air Traffic Control."

"Yes, Sir."

"I want solid information. You have eight hours. Dismissed."

The soldier saluted sharply, turned on his heel and left, almost breaking into a run before the door could close behind him.

The Colonel wanted to smile at his obedience, but he couldn't.

This was a fucking puzzle. *Who or what the hell did Clarke have on his side?*

SPARKY RAISED HIS HEAD, sprinting from the room. I didn't understand that dog and had no clue what was going on. He wasn't my dog. He owed me no loyalty.

Now I had a pack of what I assumed were his friends surrounding me and protecting me with no idea why.

I turned and looked at the monitors, more out of habit than anything else.

Just outside the gate, dogs lined both sides of the main road, facing each other. Sparky sat just inside. He turned around and looked up at the camera. His mouth moved in what could only be a bark.

I got it.

I pressed the switch that remotely lowered the gate. When it was still a dozen inches from being fully open, Sparky darted out. He looked back again from the other side and nodded at the camera.

He nodded.

A dog nodded.

I am going crazy.

I closed the gate and watched. He strode down the aisle formed by the dogs, and as he reached each pair, they lowered themselves to the dirt, bowing their heads.

Bowing in submission to the king.

My mind was broken, but the warrior was quiet. No more urges to kill, kill, kill. The dog by my side made me a new man. It made no sense at all.

And all the sense in the world.

As he reached the end of the line of mutts, Sparky turned, and I saw him bark twice. All the dogs rose to their feet and followed.

Sixty seconds later they had disappeared. Knowing he was gone, I felt lonely.

I hadn't been without him at all the last couple of days.

It felt odd, and I found myself watching the camera, waiting for his return.

———

"Wait, what?"

"There's a pack of dogs out there, Sheriff."

"Who's this?"

"I'd rather not say. But all those dogs that disappeared are running in a pack. You might have a bad case of some kind of rabies or something going around."

"Look, Mr..."

"I'm not telling you my name. Just check it out."

Just then he heard the phones start to ring out front.

"Ted!"

"I gotta go. Thanks for the tip." He hung up his personal line, wondering how the person on the other end had gotten his number.

Rushing out, he found every line lit up and ringing at once. He grabbed one.

"Sheriff Crawford."

"Sheriff, he's come back!"

"Who?"

"It's Andy. Simon is back."

"Simon?"

"My dog, Sheriff. We called that he ran off the other day."

"How is he?"

"Looks fine to me."

"Get him checked out anyway, would you?"

"Sure Sheriff, but—"

"It's on the county."

"Thanks Sheriff."

Caller after caller, after caller.

He checked them off the list and so did Alice, his dispatcher. After an hour, they compared notes.

All the dogs were back. Not one remained missing.

———

PREDATOR DRONES ARE LOUD, but they're small and hard to spot. They fly high and are relatively hard to shoot down.

None of that mattered on this mission. The pilots flew two aircraft, one flight line to the west, one to the east. They took real time photos and trained thermal cameras on the compound too. Their orders said to look for human and canine forms. A routine test of the cameras, or so they were told. Yet it was billed as a Priority One training mission.

"That's bullshit," Sergeant Elam spat.

"I know. They know the cameras can pick up and distinguish better than that."

"It's a pilot test maybe."

"What, to see how dumb we are? To test if we can fly in two parallel straight lines with no opposition, no possibility of enemy detection, and then circle a target without hitting each other. Really?"

"Just shut up and fly. Probably some top-secret cult up here, and they just don't want to tell us the real reason they're looking."

"Yeah, probably."

Silence reigned as they watched the cameras.

"Okay, target in sight. I see one human form standing right outside the doorway of the main building. You?"

"Same. Any other heat signatures?"

"Nothing."

"No dogs?"

"Nope."

"So how are we supposed to prove we can differentiate if there's nothing else there?"

"I don't know, but there's something else strange."

"What's that?"

"No wildlife in the woods."

"What do you mean?"

"The ground is cool enough, we should be picking up every-thing. Rabbits, fox, deer, birds circling around. I don't see a thing."

"Me either. Circle wider."

"Tally-ho."

"What do you have?"

"Looks like a fox, about a click out."

"Me too. A whole bunch of stuff. It's almost like..."

"Like what?"

"Like there's an invisible fence around the place, right here." He drew a circle on the map.

"Huh. Well send it up. Let's bring these birds back in."

———

I COULDN'T SEE THEM, but I heard them. It's impossible for anyone to completely hide a Predator drone. let alone two. I stood just inside the doorway and scanned the sky for movement anyway. Occasionally I found myself looking at the road.

There was still no sign of Sparky. I began to think he'd left me.

I needed to contact Marsha and then move along. I'd been in one place too long already. The arrival of the drones told me it was time to move the fight.

I'm not the one who's wrong here. I'm not the criminal. Not this time.

I didn't want to leave without Sparky. So silly. Daylight would be the best time to move, when they'd least expect it.

Then it dawned on me.

The dogs had left. Sparky led them away.

Now the drone pilots couldn't spot them. No dogs, just a single man barricaded inside the compound.

Last night amateurs brought a foolish frontal assault, but tonight they'd send in pros if they could.

I wondered if Sparky would come back, with or without his friends. Either way, I wanted to be prepared. I went out to the truck.

If I wasn't leaving yet, it was time to finish unpacking.

———

RICKY'S EARS PERKED UP, but Dale didn't hear a thing.

The dog rose and sat ready, as if waiting for a ball or stick to be thrown.

Dale sat forward in his rocker on the porch, watching with narrowed eyes. He didn't see anything at all, but Ricky's gaze seemed concentrated on the field across from the motel.

There. A red tail wagged above the weeds. Then nothing. "Ricky, come!" he commanded.

The dog glanced over at him, but looked away, gaze still focused. "Ricky!"

The Lab bolted for the front gate, leaping it easily. "Ricky!" Dale stood quickly, shouting.

But Ricky raced down the road like his ass was on fire.

Dale pounded his fist into his palm with frustration. The dog hadn't been right since last night in the woods, and now he was runnin' off for no reason.

Usually Ricky was as predictable as Christmas. Dale hurried to his truck, intending to chase him down.

———

"No dogs?"

"None."

"That makes no sense!"

"There's an anomaly, Sir."

"Yes?"

"There seemed to be an area about one kilometer in radius around the target free of wildlife altogether."

"What does that mean?"

"It's almost like there's an invisible fence, Sir."

"Any other evidence of that?"

"No, Sir. No energy sources, no unusual heat signatures. It appears the target is there alone."

"Alone?"

"Yes, Sir."

The smile was back. "Get me one squad, closest and best you can."

"Sir?"

"Tonight. One last shot at him. Then he'll move for sure."

"There's a few men I know at Lewis. Couple hours out."

"Get them."

"Sir, are you sure..."

"One last shot. Then we move on."

"May I be frank, Sir?"

"Go ahead."

"This seems personal, Sir. One guy, sitting still in the middle of nowhere in Idaho that might be recognized anywhere since he's wanted by cops and bounty hunters everywhere doesn't seem to be a threat to the Cause."

The soldier found his feet dangling from the floor, his collar bunched in the Colonel's fist, a face inches from his.

"You can speak freely, soldier, but don't ever— " a finger jabbed his chest, "—ever question my notion of the Cause and what does and does not constitute a threat. Get me those men, and let's rid ourselves of this menace once and for all."

"Yes, Sir." The fist released, and gravity took over.

"Now go."

This time the sprint started before he reached the door.

———

THE BARK STARTLED ME, and I looked up from the IED. I didn't realize I was so concentrated on my work. Either that, or he was deathly quiet.

"Hey!" I called, glad to see him. The warrior had crept back into my head while I worked, but the sight of the dog drove him away.

Sparky bounded up to me, smiling his doggy smile. He barked and wagged happily, dancing in and out of my grasp.

"Okay, okay! This is the last one."

He went to the side of the path, and sat, watching.

I finished quickly and walked the short distance back to the fence. I made my way around to the gate, and stepped inside, moving to close it. Sparky barked.

Turning back around, I saw at least fifteen dogs running up the road, every shape, size, and color.

They streamed past me into the compound, forming two evenly spaced ranks behind Sparky.

He barked once, and I closed the gate. "Better find some food for you guys, huh?"

A chorus of barks followed, and I smiled, genuinely happy for the first time since the accident.

CHAPTER TEN

"*M*r. Clarke? Mr. Clarke?"

Shaking. Goddamn that hurts! he thought. Where am I? "Mr. Clarke?"

The voice persisted, so he opened his eyes. A pretty blonde in hospital scrubs looked down at him. He opened his mouth to speak and found it dry as cotton and filled with thorns.

Water. Water would do the trick.

"Would you like a drink?"

A nod was all he could manage.

The cool glass touched his lips, and chilly heaven doused the fire in his throat. Water had never tasted so good.

"Easy! Easy!" The cup went away. He tried to sit up and chase it. The effort was too much.

"There's someone here who wants to talk to you. Do you want me to make them go away?"

"No," he managed to croak. "More water? Please?"

"Slowly. Too much will make you sick."

This time a straw touched his lips. He sucked eagerly until it disappeared. "Do you want me to send them in now?"

He shook his head. "I'll be fine." She left him staring at the celling.

Minutes passed. Then a face filled his vision. Colonel Anderson. "How are you feeling, Sergeant Clarke?"

"Not bad, considering." Fear gripped his guts, holding them in an iron vice.

"We were concerned about you. I'm glad you escaped. How did you manage that?"

He shrugged, and his shoulder erupted in flames of pain.

"Ah, well. No matter. I've come bearing gifts."

Oh, and what now? he thought.

Out loud he said, "What might that be, Sir?"

"Your discharge papers. You did a great job, but you've been made. You're of no value to the FBI or the Army anymore."

The fear rose. He didn't even know Colonel Anderson knew who he really worked for. Wasn't he the target of the investigation? Who let that nugget slip out?

"Thank you, Sir."

"You're welcome." The Colonel leaned in. "Besides that, you are nuttier than the Planter's guy. If you were to say, tell anyone some of the things that you mistakenly believe about certain members of my unit, and myself of course, no one would believe you. In fact, instead of giving you this nice disability pension, and sending you on your way, they might have you committed. And you know those mental institutions, with all those unstable patients. You never know what might happen. You never know."

His tone returned to normal as he sat back. "There's a whole Army who might want you harmed if they discovered whose side you are really on, soldier. So best of luck to you. Enjoy civilian life."

Clarke managed to raise his hands, accepting the offered paperwork and looking at it. As he did the Colonel pointed to the bottom line on his DD-214. 'Honorable,' it said.

"We wouldn't want that word to change, now would we?"

Left with no choice, he was out. Whatever happened next didn't concern him. He simply nodded, but he motioned for the Colonel to lean closer. He felt something snap in his head, and a voice not his own whispered a simple sentence.

"What's that?" the Colonel leaned in.

"It's over for now Colonel. For now."

The officer straightened almost to attention. "Best of luck, Sergeant."
He left the room without smiling, and without looking back.

———

NIGHTFALL.

The dogs were inside the compound, the warrior silent. I wasn't sure why I'd come to trust them so.

No, not them. Him. Sparky.

One dog I met only days ago somehow inspired my trust, a big word for me.

I trusted almost no one. I'd been betrayed too many times.

Sitting in the comfortable chair, I listened to the sounds of the dogs' breathing, some panting, some snoring softly as they dozed. I began to drift into sleep.

A moment later they sat up as one unit. Sparky barked, four quick snapping sounds. Together they filed out the door and down the steps.

I looked at the monitors, but didn't see a thing on any of them.

A tingle started at the base of my spine, and I steeled myself for the coming chaos of battle. When that feeling descended, I never quite felt in control. I didn't know for certain what I'd do next, only that it would somehow be the right thing. That warrior instinct had saved my life more than once.

The warrior didn't come. This time the real me, whatever that meant and whoever that was, stayed calm, cool, and ready.

The traps were set.

Whatever came next, it didn't matter. I knew I no longer had to face it alone.

———

"YOU'RE CERTAIN HE'S ALONE?"

"Yeah, positive. The predator flight is only a few hours old."

"Is now the best time?"

"He'll expect us later, or really early in the morning. If he expects us at all. He'll be resting now."

"How do you know?"

"We went through the same training. Now do me a favor."

"What's that?"

"Shut the fuck up."

"Yes, Sir."

Few people knew of their existence, let alone their capability. On a base of over 25,000 soldiers they were twelve out of a small battalion of Rangers. Anyone searching the roster of soldiers at Fort Lewis wouldn't find their names, ranks or any other information about them without the proper clearance. During his time as a covert intelligence operative, they'd been the squad Clarke was assigned to.

No one ever saw him. He rarely trained with them, and most of the men didn't even know he existed, let alone what he did, and that he was only a few miles away the entire time he did it.

The gateway to the unit was small, the number of men who stayed even smaller. Only senior NCOs stuck around. Even officers came and went with a rhythmic regularity. They had only one assignment: infiltrate and disable domestic terrorist organizations or other internal groups deemed to be a threat to national security.

Rarely, they were called out on missions like this: to handle an imminent threat. It had never before been anyone they would call one of their own gone rogue.

It made Sergeant Sylvester wonder if that was really what was going on here. Of course, more than once they'd been dispatched with no clue who the target was, or what they might or might not have done.

They told us this time, he thought, *because they didn't want us to find out on our own when we stormed in. Shock can cause you to hesitate. Hesitate around a guy with this kind of training, and you die.*

He raised the night vision goggles to his eyes. No movement, anywhere. A good sign, and a bad one.

He would have traps set. The approach would be low and slow.

In and out, no noise, the order had come down.

My specialty. He low-crawled back to where the others waited, a smile on his face. "Begin approach. Hand signals only. Radio silence. Rendezvous at the fence 2130. Clear?"

There were nods all around. The rest of the soldiers were too young, too new to really remember Clarke.

Good. If they did, they'd be scared to death.

———

MARSHA HEARD A NOISE DOWNSTAIRS, and there were never noises downstairs. Especially not tonight.

The Colonel's time was almost up, and he'd be desperate.

Desperate people do desperate things, Todd had told her.

God, she wished he was here. Here to hold her. Here to be the strong one, the one to respond to any threat.

But he wasn't. He'd taught her to defend herself, both armed and unarmed, almost as if he'd known this day might come at a point when she was threatened and alone.

The pink handle was the only feminine thing about her Taurus PT25. Slowly, silently she headed down the stairs with it at the ready. A rattle came from the kitchen, near the back door. Nowhere anyone should be this time of night.

As she slowly eased her weight down on each tread, careful not to make them creak, avoiding gripping the handrail, not too close to the wall so the smooth silk of her shirt brushing the plaster would not alert anyone below that she was on the way, the noises stopped just as suddenly as they'd begun. She paused, four steps from the bottom, listening.

Nothing.

Absolute silence. Either the intruder had moved further into the house, and was suddenly stealthier, or they'd panicked and left. She knew they hadn't found what they were looking for. One of her copies of the letter was in the downstairs office. The other was in a safe behind a painting in the bedroom.

What she'd told the Colonel about other copies wasn't a complete ruse: there was one other copy in the safety deposit box at her bank. It would likely be found in the event of her death, but it might take days or weeks for her parents and attorneys to sort their way through her things and figure out what they had.

Her heart beat in her ears, and she took a deep breath, trying to slow it down. Still no sounds came from below.

She eased down the next step. And the next. Two more, and she was standing on the landing in the living room. The noises had come from her left. To the right was a short hallway that led to the downstairs office and the front door.

Mentally, she flipped a coin, and chose to go left. Edging off the landing, she followed the wall, staring into the darkness that was the center of the room. Nothing moved. In a drawer in the table, halfway down the hall, a small flashlight rested. She quietly slid the drawer open, and dropped the hard cylinder into the pocket of her pajama pants. Just as carefully, she slid it shut.

The light was for later, just in case. *Don't ruin your night vision. Use it to ruin theirs,* she heard Todd explain in her head.

"I will," she whispered, wishing again for his presence. Sliding along the wall, she drew close to the opening that led to the downstairs bathroom. Bypassing it quickly, she edged around the kitchen doorway, and looked inside.

No one was there. The light had a dimmer, and so she turned the knob barely, illuminating every corner.

Nothing.

She'd heard something, now knowing she had not imagined it.

Then it came again. A soft scratching at the back door. Down low.

She hadn't had a dog since she was a kid, but it sounded like one scratching to be let in. The knob rattled, claws scratching on either side of it. It couldn't be.

Surely the dog wasn't trying to open the door?

Slowly she made her way around the table, flipped on the porch light and peeked through the blinds. She couldn't see anyone. Looking down as low as she could, she realized she couldn't see a thing closer than the first step. There could be a dog there, or a man, imitating a dog, sitting very close to the door.

As quietly as she could, she eased back the dead bolt, hearing an urgent whine as she did.

Slowly she eased the door open. A medium sized mongrel pushed it open, out of her hand, causing her to cry out.

The door swung wider, headed for impact with the wall. The dog was quicker, around the door like a flash, swinging it closed. The pooch stood on his hind legs, his paws on either side of the door, looking up at the lock. He barked once, a near whisper if that was even possible.

Marsha reached out, shooting the bolt home.

The dog plopped down on all fours, and then she got a good look at him.

Long scraggly black fur and droopy ears framed a kind face. An arrow of white and gray fur decorated the chest, and he wagged his tail.

He didn't wear a collar, but there was a mussed line of fur where one had rested not long ago and by the look of it for an extended stay.

Marsha moved warily forward, and the dog closed its mouth, stopping its panting tongue for a moment, cocking his head as if listening closely. He lowered his head with canine respect, stretching his neck out.

Go ahead, pet me, he seemed to say.

She reached out, scratching him behind the ears, rubbing his head. The strange dog responded enthusiastically, dancing about her kitchen with giddy excitement, but not barking.

Marsha giggled as he did. Strange, but even with this dog showing up unannounced at her house in the middle of the night, she felt oddly at ease.

He smelled though, like the dog she remembered from her childhood when he'd gone off running or been playing really hard and needed a bath. The dog was sweaty, and thirsty. His tongue hung from his mouth, but no drool fell from it. She found an old metal bowl in the cupboard, and filled it, setting it gently on the floor.

He quickly dropped his head, lapping eagerly.

She smiled again, wishing for the umpteenth time that Todd was here to share this, the oddest of moments.

The front doorbell rang.

The dog took off before she had a chance, barking fiercely, his tail no longer wagging.

Marsha followed close behind, wondering who could be at her door so late at night.

———

INCHES AT A TIME, the men crept forward. Two claymores were disabled. One pressure mine marked, but not disabled. They had no time for that.

He was impressed with the men. If nothing else, this was good training. Clarke was making it easy. He had almost reached the fence, and the rendezvous point.

Another twenty feet. The dirt was loose here. Closer to the fence the ground was covered gravel that would make noise if they stepped on it.

Sergeant Sylvester looked right and left. Shapes made their way slowly toward the gate. This would be the pinch point, but he had a code, so opening it won't be a problem, as long as it hadn't been changed.

As soon as we open the gate, he'll know we're here. Once he knows, we better move, or we'll be in trouble.

He slid his right leg forward, intending to crawl the last few feet, and then move right toward the gate. As he did, he heard a nearly inaudible click. He stopped, motionless.

Moving now might be deadly. He held absolutely still, and then slowly raised his hand as far as he could, hoping someone was looking his way. He wagged it right and left.

Come to me, it meant.

He waited, not hearing a sound. Even the crickets were quiet. No birds chirped. The night held its collective breath.

Reached his hand up again, careful not to move his leg. Wagged again. Come to me.

He heard the rustle of clothing and cursed. He looked straight ahead through the fence. For a moment he glimpsed a pair of yellow eyes surrounded by fur. He blinked, and they were gone.

A second later he felt a gentle tap on his shoulder. "You okay, Sarge?" A voice whispered.

"No. I triggered something. Right leg. I'm afraid to move. Check it out."

Other shapes came closer.

"Spread those goddamn men out," he said. "Get me two here to help me, the rest, spread the hell out!"

He heard movement as they obeyed his hushed command.

The Sergeant, barely 35, but a veteran of many missions, breathed in and out very slowly. Things felt bad. Very bad.

He heard a low, sharp intake of breath from one of the soldiers behind him. "Sergeant?"

"Yeah?"

"It's a pressure-triggered IED. A big one."

"Can you disable it?"

"I don't know. I can try."

"Okay then."

A low growl came from the rear and to his left. Not from the other side of the fence, but from behind them.

He heard a scream. Then another. He craned his head around trying his best not to move.

Something struck his right side, hard.

Another click sounded, louder than the first. Beside his right knee, a fire started, a tiny glow of orange. It lasted a fraction of a second.

It lasted an hour. His last hour, as he felt himself lifted from the ground and thrown against the fence. Needles and knife blades entered his chest, his arms, and his face. He hung above the ground, hovering for an indeterminate time, able to look around, to register his surroundings. Two men were screaming, their clothes on fire.

Gunfire, muzzle flashes sent bullets through the holes in the chain link fence and into the compound.

Barking. There were so many dogs barking.

Then his orbit ended, escape velocity never reached, and he fell through the atmosphere back to the earth with a jolt.

Then nothing.

CHAPTER ELEVEN

*H*ours *in the gym had made the limp hardly noticeable. His physical therapist had told him it would be gone before he knew it.*

Still, he was glad he was standing up front, and didn't have to walk anywhere. He would have fallen over.

The dress swept his breath from his lungs.

A moment later, she stood before him, shoulders bare, a thin veil hardly disguising her happiness and enthusiasm.

"Todd, do you take this woman to be your lawfully wedded wife, to have and to hold, in sickness and in health, in happiness and sorrow, for richer or poorer, until death do you part?"

"I do."

"And do you Marsha?"

She did.

The wedding was huge, the party enormous, a sea of strangers offering their congratulations, shaking hands, hugging. Drink after drink found its way into his hand, and down his throat.

Late. The crowd started to disperse. Tomorrow they would leave on their honeymoon. Their early departure times ensured he would be plagued with a hangover.

Someone appeared at his elbow.

"Sergeant Clarke?"

"Not anymore."

"Take this, Sergeant."

A hand, slipping something inside his jacket pocket. A thin package.

Never again. He'd promised. Turning around to see who'd invaded his wedding day with this indecent and unwelcome thing, he saw no one.

Sliding the contents from the stiff envelope, he found a card, half of a $100 bill, and a note.

"Best wishes", the card read in fancy script. The note inside was short, hand written.

"I know even a married man can keep secrets." Underneath was a scrawled signature: Colonel Mike Anderson.

Put it in your wallet, the warrior had commanded. He only heard it in the gym and the physical therapy office, when he was fighting his own body.

Obedience wasn't a question. He folded the note around the half-bill and put both in his wallet.

Marsha was there, arms around his neck, the scent of perfume and sweat filling his senses. She kissed him, and he tasted sweet wine mixed with cake.

"Take me to bed," she commanded.

He did.

———

MARSHA EASED her way to the door, gun in hand. The new addition to her life barked with increasing fury at the door. The knocking stopped, and she heard muffled voices.

Then it started again. A steady pounding. "Mrs. Clarke? It's about your husband."

She stayed silent. The dog continued to bark, and she couldn't think.

"Shut up!" she hissed. The dog closed his mouth for a second and then looked at her, panting.

What next? his look said.

Good question.

Time for some acting, but not too much.

"Who is it?" She tried to sound groggy and half-asleep, and thought she mostly succeeded.

Muffled conversation. The dog growled, deep in his throat, and she shushed him. "FBI ma'am."

"Got any ID? My husband always taught me to ask for ID."

"Sure ma'am, if you could just open the door." There was a pause. "And control your dog."

Funny, she wasn't sure she could comply with that one. She looked down at the mutt, and smiled. "You'll protect me, right?"

He looked up at her and barked.

"I'll take that as a yes." Slipping the pistol into the pocket of her robe, she opened the door a hair.

It flew back on its hinges striking the wall. The first man through the door shoved her back, and she fell sprawling.

She watched with disbelief as the dog attacked.

He leapt off his haunches and locked his jaws on the man's extended forearm. The man screamed and a huge gun fell from his hand, striking the carpet near her. It looked like Todd's Desert Eagle .45. She scrambled backward, leaving it. It was too big for her to handle accurately, so she pulled her own pistol and searched for a clear shot.

A second assailant followed the first. He assumed a careful stance and fired. The shot ended her hearing other than a long high ringing. She saw the dog release the man's wrist and fly toward her, landing in her lap. The canine body knocked her pistol from her hand, and it slid across the floor. The man followed the dog, staring at the huge hole in his fur. Blood flowed into a puddle between her legs.

She screamed, but heard nothing. The dog's mouth opened in a howl, ending with his tongue hanging from the side of his mouth, ears laid back against his skull. His eyes darted back and forth, limbs twitching as he attempted to move, to run away.

Scrambling onto her belly, she crawled for her fallen gun. The mixed scent of sulfur and the freshly spilled blood made her nauseous. Still unable to hear, she inched forward. A second later, she felt a hand on her shoulder.

A stern face with close-set eyes, wearing lips set in an angry line greeted her. The man raised his fist, punching her in the face. Her nose broke, blood flowed into her mouth and over her chin. Unable to stop herself, she retched and bent to the side emptying the contents of her stomach on to the carpet. Retching a second time, her ears popped, and she could hear again.

What she heard astounded her. First a growl, a manly scream, and then the sound of a gunshot.

There was the tiniest pause, and then she saw the body of the dog land beside her, this time clearly dead, heard the wet plop as what remained of his head struck the floor.

Then she heard two more gunshots in rapid succession. Followed by two more. Something heavy and soft struck her, knocking the wind from her lungs.

She struggled to get out from under it, to see what was going on, and to reach the body of the dog who had so selflessly defended her. Screaming and sobbing, all the strength left her. Surrendering, she fell to the floor, wailing in frustration.

A second later the weight was lifted from her and she was blinded by beautiful, white light.

THE EXPLOSION ROCKED THE NIGHT, and I searched the monitors. There, number three.

That explosion had ruined anyone outside's night vision. Time to go see for myself, but carefully.

The first sound that reached my ears was screaming mixed with barking. The smell was horrid. Fuel, fertilizer, blood. I moved along the side of the building toward the dying fire.

What I saw as I rounded the corner blew my mind. I stepped from cover without thinking.

The rattle of gunfire woke me from my momentary stupor, and I stepped back, carefully looking around the stone wall.

They weren't shooting at me. I heard a whine of pain followed by more barking, and another blood-curdling scream. It grabbed my spine, and propelled me into the open, the need to see what was happening urgent.

A body lay right outside the fence. Dressed in combat fatigues and riddled with holes, its right leg was gone.

Two other badly burned bodies were visible. Screams and howls came from deeper in the woods. At the ready, in the shadows, stood a dozen mutts, all watching carefully, hackles up. For a moment flames crackled as a nearby bush burned.

A wounded dog appeared, crawling toward the fence, bleeding from a wound on its right flank, panting heavily.

A head slid under my hand, and I looked down to find Sparky inexplicably at my side. Had he not gone out with the others? I scratched his ears absent-mindedly, and he looked up at me, barking sharply.

"Sure, boy." Opening the gate, immediate danger seemed unlikely. An army of dogs protected me, and there were booby traps all over the place. My current assailants seemed to be on the run.

When the code was entered, the gate slid away. I pulled my pistol, more out of habit than need. Sparky stayed by my side as I exited, and glancing back, I saw all but two of the mutts follow us into the night, scattering silently in all directions. Two that took up posts guarding the gate looked like the same Doberman mixes who had guarded the road before.

Security team alpha, the MPs of our little band.

Some of the dogs had started to look familiar. I liked them all, and the security I felt having them on my side. I'd never been a dog person. *What's going on with me?*

I turned toward the scene of the explosion. Only a few yards from the gate, I saw the signs of gore. Then I saw the body.

It lay face down, the right leg missing below the thigh, a large puddle of blood where the limb used to be. The back of the uniform was filled with bloody holes. He must have been right on top of the bomb. A bloody body print decorated the chain link way up high. I turned him over.

My eyes widened for a moment. I recognized him. Fucking Sylvester. A good soldier, as I remembered.

What the hell is he doing here? Fucking Anderson probably sent him.

Sparky moved next to the wounded dog beside the fence. A Lab mix, he panted heavily, lying on his side. He tried to pick his head up as I approached, but it fell to the graveled earth. His right flank looked like raw steak. A ribbon of fur and flesh was missing from halfway down his back to just above his tail. I knelt to get a closer look.

The edges of the wound were ragged. I wouldn't be able to stitch it, but the bleeding wasn't too bad. A scab, rough and ugly, had already formed. Clotted blood stuck in the fur around the wound. I'd noticed collars on a few of the dogs, and he wore one, red nylon with a hoop to attach a leash and a tag.

"Ricky," I read aloud. "Good boy Ricky." I gently patted his head, and his tail wagged once. He whimpered. Sparky sat near his head, running his tongue noisily in and out of his mouth.

"I think he'll be okay," I told him.

He seemed relieved, but turned his head, right to left, eyes active, never focusing on any one thing. A good strategy for any guard. My lookout, that's what his job was.

Engraved under the name Ricky was "Dale," no last name, a Boise address and phone number. I debated what to do.

I'd be safe for a few hours, but Anderson would be short on options. A lone clandestine assassin, private soldiers, now a military strike. He had to be down to the limits of his reach. He'd try to destroy the compound, using who knew what means. If we stuck around, we'd be dead. Time to get out of Dodge.

I needed a vet.

A moan sounded from off to my left, away from the fence, and I looked over, startled. "I'll be back, boy." I patted Ricky gently on the head and received a limp tail wag in return.

Sparky stayed next to him, and I moved toward the sound. One of the charred bodies moved.

He wasn't on top of the bomb, like the dead soldier, but I wouldn't call him lucky. His body was riddled with shrapnel and severely charred. His fatigues had mostly burned from his flesh. The laces of his left boot appeared to have been ripped apart by a giant hand, the foot hung on the bottom of his leg at an odd angle, his ankle clearly broken.

His breath struggled in and out of his ruined throat with a hissing rasp. In the faint starlight filtering through the trees, I could see his right eye was swollen shut, cheek black and blue, nose shattered. The uninjured eye darted around, settling on me as I knelt by his side.

I'd seen worse, but he'd be dead without quick medical attention. I wondered if the dogs had left anyone else alive. If so, the survivors would be reporting back to Anderson soon. He probably already had a plan in place just in case this squad wasn't successful. How much time did I have?

None.

No time to rescue both the soldier and the wounded dog. Clearly Ricky would live, if I could get him some help.

I would have given the soldier a 10% chance.

Not even really a choice; I raised my pistol, letting him see it. He raised a weak hand.

I fired, one shot to the head. He stopped moaning, stopped moving.

Moving back toward the compound, I needed to make a litter for Ricky and get moving. If I hesitated, there would only be one end to this for all of us.

Death.

———

THE SOLDIER CREPT on his belly through the brush. He nearly cried out at the shot, but somehow managed to stay silent. There was no other way to survive. The dog. The dog was more likely to sense him, his smell, his sounds, his movements, more so than the man.

He smelled of blood and exploded flesh, gunpowder, piss, and shit. In other words, dead, at least to himself. Everyone he'd seen was dead. Carter was missing, but that could mean anything.

He'd been bitten hard on his calf and left forearm, and lost a lot of blood. The dog had moved on when he'd played dead. He was lucky, maybe.

Two rounds remained in his weapon, one for the man, one for the dog that stayed by his side. It was all he had, all he needed.

The guy shot Adams. Right in the face. Sure, he was dying, and maybe it was a mercy.

But he left that dog alive.

"C'mon Sparky," he heard. "We'll be back, Ricky."

Waiting until they were out of sight, he crawled forward, selecting what he hoped was a better position. Stabilizing his weapon on a rock, he set up a sight picture near the fallen dog. It panted, occasionally whacking its tail on the packed gravel.

Stay calm. Patience.

A truck engine started up from inside the compound, and he thought he might not have to wait long after all.

———

RAY WHISTLED AS HE DROVE. "I Fell in a Pile of You and Got Love All Over Me" played on the radio. His hat sat on the seat next to him.

Some folks called him narrow minded, but he told 'em he liked both kinds of music, Country and Western, and both types of politicians, conservative and fundamentalist. His religious views were Baptist, and a King James Bible peeked out from under his hat. A Regan/Bush '84 sticker covered a rust spot on the tailgate of his aging Dodge pickup, and he hadn't really liked a damn president since. The other side bore a Batt for Governor sticker, and he held similar sentiment about the leadership of his state: the 80's were a good time for politicians in his book.

If you'd listen, he'd tell you how much better job a regular guy like him would do, if given a shot at the big offices, but he'd never even run for Mayor or County Commissioner. Hell, he'd never even run for the school board.

The only reason he was goin' into town was that his wife was outta Foldger's and she got even bitchier when she didn't have her morning coffee. He could use some Redman too, while he was there, but his wife had heard he was going, and handed him a list that promised to shoot his morning all to hell.

His dog Travis Tritt, named for the Country singer of course, rode in the back. He loved that dog, but he'd be damned if he was gonna ride in the cab smelling like that. His longish hair, inherited from one of the unknown breeds in his ancestry, made weekly baths a necessity for the farm dog, but bath day wasn't 'til tomorrow, and God knew his wife wouldn't do a damn thing early.

The last coupla' days had been odd. Loud, plane-like engines, but nothin' he could see, a coupla' choppers before that, and the howlin'. That was the worst.

He kept his dogs inside at night, somethin' Travis Tritt in the back there was none too fond of, but all the action outside had made him nervous.

The coyotes had never bothered him much, but this was a different kinda howlin'. It wasn't normal, and he'd been listening to the woods up here for his entire life. He knew when something was wrong, and this was for sure one of those times. As if to emphasize his point, a mutt ran across the road, damn near right at his bumper. He slammed on his brakes, the rubber of his mismatched used tires slipped on the dirt and loose gravel. Looking curiously after the dog, he inched forward.

Travis let out a sharp bark, and he turned his attention forward just in time.

A man staggered out of the woods into the middle of the road holding a pistol and fired it at the fleeing dog.

Ray slammed his foot into the brake pedal for the second time in a coupla' minutes, sending a wail of protest into the air from the rusty, grooved rotors. The sound of metal on metal told him what he already knew: his brake pads were way overdue for replacement. The man stood panting in the center of the road, oblivious to the iron and steel sliding his way.

"Ha! Ha!" He shouted and then turned. "Oh shit!"

Ray saw the words form on the man's lips and tugged the wheel hard to the right, trying his damndest not to run this fool down.

The truck slid to a stop mere inches from the man's knees. It rocked back onto the rear springs in protest of its recent abuse, and Ray killed the engine.

The man in front of him wore a military uniform of some sort, more modern than the one Ray remembered from the time he'd served. His cover was gone, and a reddish brown stain obscured the name printed above his left breast pocket. He raised his pistol, pointing it through the windshield.

"Hands up!"

"Hey there," Ray greeted.

"Hands! Show me your fucking hands, now!"

"Take it easy." Ray raised his hands, leaning his head out the window, puzzled. "You look hurt bud. How can I help ya'?"

"You got a cell phone?"

"No, Sir. I never got one of them, and they hardly work out here anyway. Can I give you a lift somewhere?"

"Who are you?"

"Name's Ray. I live just up there a ways. One of the only houses around these parts. I can take you there, get you cleaned up." He held out his hand, hoping to put this soldier at ease. Looked like if he couldn't, he might end up shot.

"No. Gimme your truck."

"Now hold on."

"No. Slide on out, and walk away."

"Son, I ain't gonna do that."

The soldier looked uncertain, then raised his weapon again. "Get out."

"Nope. Wanna know why?"

"I'm runnin' outta time, so you better talk fast, and tell me why I shouldn't shoot you, and take your truck anyway."

"'Cause you're hurt, and I can get you where you're going. Without me, you seem likely to crack this rig up, and end up dead on one of these country roads. Doubt you know your way. Could end up lost."

"Why should I trust you?"

"I was a soldier once, son. And this here truck's got some quirks, least that's what I call 'em. My wife won't drive her. You probably shouldn't try in your current state." The tip of the pistol lowered a little, and then Travis growled from the bed.

The pistol came up again. "That there's another reason," Ray continued. "I don't know why you were shootin' at that dog, but you don't seem to be a fan of canines. Travis here might not take kindly to you shootin' me, or tryin' to take my truck anywhere without me."

"Will he bite me?"

"Not 'less I tell him to."

The tip of the pistol dropped, and the soldier staggered, nearly falling to the road. Ray noticed the red stain on his shoulder. It looked fresh, and it was spreading.

"Son, quit wastin' your time and mine. Looks like you could use a doc. Hop on in, and I'll drive ya'."

"Help..." The man nearly fell.

Ray rushed to his side and slipped the pistol from his hand. Now wasn't the time for a firearm accident. He checked the safety one-handed with the sure experience of one who knew his weapons, and slid the gun into the back of his jeans, under the carved leather that both bore his name and kept his pants from slipping south.

"C'mon son," he said, assisting the injured man into the passenger seat.

Travis reached his head out to be scratched when he moved to close the door, and he obliged.

Good damn dog. I wonder why this young man was shootin' at a dog, 'specially one runnin' from him.

Ray slammed the door and switched his CB to channel nine. It'd be a bit before he'd be in range to rouse anyone, but givin' the docs a heads up seemed like a good idea.

Besides, bringing in an injured soldier from the woods around here? Should earn him the right to know what the hell was goin' on.

At least that's the way he saw it.

The cassette clicked, flippin' to the other side of the funny songs tape he put in this mornin'.

The lovely strains of "If my Nose was Runnin' Money, I'd Blow it all Over You" poured from the long worn out factory speakers with now familiar static.

The soldier closed his eyes, clearly resting for the first time in a long time. Under the dried blood, he could just make out the last name "Carter" and notes his rank: E-6. Staff sergeant if he remembered right.

What are you doing here? He wondered as he shifted the truck into drive, whistling along to the music. Maybe today wouldn't be quite so dull after all.

CHAPTER TWELVE

"What do you mean, a noble sacrifice?" The tattoo artist paused in his work, an intricate design subtly incorporating the number twelve. With his job, it would be inadvisable to have displayed his personal sentiment so blatantly on his body, but the eighty eight hidden in the lion's head on his left bicep just didn't feel like enough.

"Abram was willing to sacrifice Isaac. God provided a substitute."

Placing his arm back on the arm of the chair, he gripped the pad. "Continue," he told the artist and Colonel Anderson at the same time.

"I have a proposal to rid ourselves of a problem, before the Big Day."

"No one outside the organization will be able to track anything back to us."

"Almost no one."

The artist stopped when he moved his arm again.

"Take five," the tattooee ordered. The artist nodded, and grabbed a pack of smokes off the table, tossing his rubber gloves on his way out.

"You mean Clarke," he said as the door closed.

"Yeah."

"He's untouchable, you know that. Anything happens to him, and you'll...we'll be first on the suspect list."

"I know. I have an idea, but it's elaborate."

"Go ahead."

"It would involve you giving up some things."

"Like what?"

"You and Tyler in witness protection. Likely out of the country, at least temporarily. New identities. That part would be permanent."

"You're kidding."

"Nope. Give up the job, and likely never see this place again."

"That has plusses and minuses. His mother..."

"Will believe the cover story. Everyone will."

"So we'll be dead."

"As far as anyone will know."

"What else?"

"It'll take resources..."

"How much?"

"All the organization has."

"In return?"

"Fifteen million."

"Fifteen?"

"Best I can do."

"Tell me the idea."

"How in is Tyler?"

"He's as sold out to the Cause as I am."

"Okay then. We need a couple of his friends, and a proper substitute."

"Colonel..."

"Leave the details to me, just be ready. Tell your people I need their full cooperation, no questions asked. The fewer people that know the whole plan, the better."

"I'll tell them. What next?"

"Meet me here, tomorrow at six. Bring Tyler, the names of his friends, and a list of who we have in local law enforcement, ambulance, and tow trucks. Anyone who might respond to an accident."

"Mike, what are you planning?"

"I'll fill you in tomorrow. Until then."

Mike stood, slapping the incomplete tattoo as hard as he could.

"Ouch, you fuck!"

"See you tomorrow, brother." As he left he saluted, right fist over heart first, then halfway out from his chest, stiff and formal.

He received a raised middle finger in return but knew the man would do as he asked. Hell, he almost had no choice.

———

"I'M GETTIN' nervous."

"He said he'd call, but maybe he can't."

"When can we get the money?"

"When we get the fucking call."

"I don't want to wait."

"Shut up, Tommy. Too soon, someone figures out we got paid off. They start asking questions, look too close, find out we lied, and we're all dead."

"Easy for you to say. Your parents have money. You get nice shit anyway. I'm due a nice chunk of change, I saw a new Plan B board the other day, and I can't even afford that! C'mon man."

"I'll spot you a hundred. Just keep a lid on it, okay."

"Yeah, all right. But I'm tired of waiting."

"Just chill a little longer."

"Okay. Hey, thanks for the loan. I'll pay it back as soon as we get our money. First thing outta my share."

"It's a gift. Don't worry about it."

Exchanging high fives, the younger teen walked away.

"I'm worried about him, Jed."

"I know, Will, I know."

"I'm getting kind of anxious myself."

"We all are, but just chill. Tyler never let us down before."

"Yeah, but the big guy with him gave me the creeps. Some kind of soldier or something."

"His dad was on the level though. Just into all that White Power shit, but other than that, he was cool."

"Okay, but I still think we should use the card."

"I don't think Tommy counts as an emergency yet, but if it gets to that point, I'll make the call."

"You're the man, Jed."

Will walked a couple of steps, then put his board down, skating quickly away.

Jed opened his cell phone and fingered the keys. To call, or not to call. He keyed in the nine digits, followed by the instructed four-digit extension.

"Yes?" A voice answered.

"Um, I was told to call this number."

"I'm aware of who gave you this number and why. What's the nature of your emergency?"

All business. No need to beat around the bush. "Tommy is nervous. Asking about the money. We're all getting anxious actually."

"The deal is you don't get it until the call."

"I know that, but Tommy doesn't want to wait. Maybe if you let him have some of it."

"None of it, until you get the call."

"Understood."

"Be sure Tommy gets the message. I'd hate for anyone else to have to deliver it."

"Okay."

"Anything else?"

"No."

A click. That simple. Make sure he gets the message. A threat, loud and clear.

The whole thing was fucked. He debated sending Tommy a text. Nah, the hun would hold him over until tomorrow. Give him a chance to cool down. He could text him in the morning.

Sliding the phone into his pack, and grabbing his board, a Zero and a true beaut, he pushed off down the street, not looking back.

———

THE DOG APPEARED FIRST. Wagging its tail, running ahead. The guy appeared next, still armed, but his pistol secure in a holster. A truck sat outside the gate, and he thought of shooting for that, but it was a bit far: besides he only had two rounds. No, better to use them on flesh and blood targets.

Watching, he breathed as shallowly and silently as he could, allowing himself a little smile through the pain when the guy, carrying two five-foot poles with cloth rolled around them under his arm, laughed at the dog's enthusiasm.

A little closer buddy, just a little closer.

Sweat ran into his eyes, stinging, and he shook his head the tiniest bit to clear his vision. The dog went from jovial to on guard, instantly staring straight at his position.

The mutt stood, legs apart and aggressive, a low growl coming from his throat. The guy dropped the stretcher and pulled his pistol.

"What is it, boy?"

No time left. With his vision still blurry and an imperfect sight picture, he pulled the trigger. The rifle bucked back against his shoulder and he heard a muffled "oof."

Then the dog was on him, biting. He felt its teeth sink into his shoulder, and then his neck. His hand twitched in reflex, discharging his second and final round.

As he passed from this world into the next, his finger spasmed on the trigger, over and over.

Click, click, click, click, click. The last thing he heard was a firing pin striking an empty chamber.

———

MY LEG. Fuck, my leg.

My calf was bleeding. Shit! Not bad though, just grazed. It needed stitches, but fuck that. There was no time, no time.

At Sparky's feet a body lay, neck bitten open, blood pumping out in spurts. The dog panted heavily.

"Come!"

The dog did. A barrel pointed at the sky, and I heard a faint click. It slid downward, and the rifle clattered into the dirt. Sparky ran over, barking.

Did I do good?

"Yeah, you did good boy." My gaze shifted to the dog we came back to rescue. Its head was gone. The final shot must've struck him. Sparky wandered over, circled around the dog, and then whined at me.

Jesus this sucks.

Turning to walk away, I put weight on my ankle, forgetting my injury for a moment.

Time to patch up. Sitting down, I unrolled the makeshift stretcher. Pulling my knife from its sheath on my side, I cut two longish strips from the cloth that made up the center. I grabbed a branch and tied the first strip of material around my leg above the knee. Making a half-knot I inserted the stick and completed the knot above it, twisting it two or three times. Good enough to slow the blood.

My hands trembled as I cut a square from the blanket. Not the most sanitary bandage, but I had to be able to move.

If that soldier survived, maybe someone else did too.

Forming the square into a ball, I stuffed it in the center of the wound where it was the deepest. I wrapped the second strip around it, tight, applying constant pressure. I needed water, needed to stay hydrated. I also needed a doctor. A vet would probably do. I took one of the poles I used to make the litter, and, using it as a cane, I made my way to the truck.

As I did, I found myself crying for Ricky, at least enough that my eyes were moist. Another fallen soldier in my life. I'd seen so many fall. So many.

That dog was just the latest to sacrifice his life for me. I wiped my eyes, throwing the makeshift cane into the back. Sparky hopped into the passenger seat. He too seemed quiet, as if he shared my thoughts.

Time to make a call, and get the hell away from here, now just another place of death.

———

"Sheriff Crawford."

"Colonel, you want to fill me in?"

"Fill you in on what?"

"I have a bloody soldier in my office who will only give his message to you. He said something about death and dogs. Then he shut up."

"Let me speak to him."

"Not until you tell me what's going on."

"What do you mean, Sheriff?"

"Don't act innocent with me. I have dogs disappearing and reappearing. Bodies around an old Aryan compound, soldiers coming and going, bodies that I'm told not to worry about. Well, I'm worrying about them. If something's going on in my jurisdiction, I want to know what it is."

"I told you already. We're hunting a dangerous fugitive who skipped bail."

"I know, Todd Clarke. That doesn't justify or explain this."

"I was going to say who may also be a threat to national security and has become a high priority government target. Now let me talk to my soldier."

"We're not done yet, Colonel."

"We are for now."

"Fine. Here he is."

The sheriff handed the phone to the wounded man, sitting stubbornly on a wheeled gurney in an exam room in the Syringa hospital. He listened for a moment.

"I'm the only one I know of. Yes, Sir, I could, but I don't think it would do any good."

"Yes, Sir."

The Sheriff stepped away, opening his own cell phone. "Yes," a female voice answered on the first ring.

"Bobbie Ann, can you come meet me right away?"

"Takes me damn near four hours to get there."

"The way you drive, honey? See you in three and a half, at the café?"

"This better be good, Ted."

"Maybe the story of the century."

"Sure."

She hung up, and he headed back to the soldier, who handed him the phone as he stepped over.

"Good news Sheriff."

"Really? That's a switch for you. What is it Colonel?"

"Mr. Clarke has left your area. We won't be bothering you anymore."

"Why don't I believe you?"

"Believe or not, now we're done."

The line went dead. Fuck that. True or not, he was handing the story to Bobbie. Let her make of it what she could.

————

Colonel Anderson ended the call, not ashamed at all of the lie he'd just told. It would be true soon enough. Either Clarke would run, or he'd be dead.

He dialed another number. "Yes?" A voice answered.

"Blow it, and then we're done."

"Sir?"

"You heard me. Now."

"Yes, Sir."

The call ended and he only hesitated for a moment before making another one.

"Yes?" Another almost mechanical voice on the end of another powerful line.

"Plan Charlie. Go."

"Yes, Sir."

Colonel Mike Anderson hung up and did something he hadn't done since his days in Catholic school. He crossed himself.

God have mercy on my soul.

————

"W HAT'S HAPPENING, S HERIFF?"

"I can't tell you."

"C'mon."

"Ray, no offense, but your wife has a mouth the size of Wyoming. I tell you and you let anything slip, the President will know what's going on here before dinner."

"What if I don't go home?"

"Huh?"

"What if I stay here, and help you out?"

"What?"

"You know, like a deputy or something. You sure look like you need help."

"Ray."

"Yeah?"

"Go home."

"If you say so." Ray filed out, and Sheriff Crawford wondered, not for the first time, if he was doing the right thing bringing Bobbie Ann into this. Too late now. Once he'd given that bloodhound the scent, nothing would throw her off, other than a bigger story. He sat down at his desk, looking at his watch. Two hours max.

He made notes, deciding exactly what he'd tell her.

CHAPTER THIRTEEN

*"*He lives a ways out huh?"

"Yeah. We do it here. Very little traffic, and he's an early mover."

"So close it here?" He motioned to the map.

"Yeah."

"First responders?"

"Quick but not too quick."

"Close both sides?"

"Yeah. This side for about 20 minutes. The other? About the same. By the time it reopens, the accident will close it again."

"You think he'll buy it?"

"Yeah."

"You think he'll react like you want?"

"I'm sure he will."

"How do you know?"

"It's what I would do."

"THIS IS WILSON." Silence. "Wilson."

"Wilson, fuck, it's Clarke."

125

"What's going on?"

"I need a doc, man, and we need to get the fuck out of here."

"Easy, man. What happened?"

"I held off two assaults at the compound."

"Why didn't you leave after the first one? Are you out of your mind?"

"Maybe. Maybe in it for the first time in a long time. It's a long story. Listen, I can drive out of here, but I need a doc sooner rather than later."

"Let me make some calls. Wait, did you say we?"

"Yeah. Me and my new dog."

"The dog still?"

"Long story. I'm on a sat phone I acquired. Call you back when I can. One more thing."

"Yeah?"

"How's Marsha?"

"I'll get her tonight. Gotta get to work here."

"Wilson?"

"What?"

"Thanks man."

"You're welcome."

———

"Did you catch that signal?"

"Yes, Sir."

"He's still there?"

"Looks like it. Or someone else using a sat phone."

"Thought I taught him better than that. Can you tell who he called?"

"No, Sir."

"Catch any of the conversation?"

"No, Sir. It's one of our encrypted phones."

"You can't listen to our own phones?"

"That's the idea, Sir. No one can."

"How far out is Delta Foxtrot?"

"Twenty minutes, Sir."

"Roger that. Plan Charlie?"

"Underway, Sir. But I have to caution you..."

"What?"

"General Malden is poking around. He doesn't seem to have anything concrete, but he's asking about certain recently allocated resources."

Colonel Mike Anderson stood. The world was changing, moving on, and not the way he liked at all. Maybe this should be his last operation. Maybe he should retire after this, if his career was still intact, and if he still could.

Or maybe he should just go for broke, and afterward just disappear.

The Brethren were scattered. The country he had sworn to serve was becoming an abomination, a blight on the Promised Land, an offense in the eyes of the Lord. One last time, he could wake the people to their transgressions, to what the inferior races were doing to pollute this land, not to mention the sexual deviants, now accepted by the military.

Yes, it's time to leave, he thought. *But it's time to leave with a bang.*

One dead. Clarke.

By the end of the week, a whole bunch of other dead folks too.

The rest of the soldiers who followed him in this endeavor? *Fuck them. If they're committed to the Cause, to the vision of a New World, they'll follow. If not, they'll fry anyway. Collateral damage, the kind he could live with.*

"Proceed anyway. If the General wants to sniff around, let him. By the time he knows what's really going on, this will be over."

"Yes, Sir."

He could tell by the little smile that this soldier was one of the chosen few. He moved out of earshot and made a call.

"Sir."

"Gather the Brethren. Plan Charlie activated."

"How many?"

"Everyone."

"How soon?"

"I want them here tomorrow."

"The usual place?"

"No. Sending coordinates now."

"Yes, Sir."

Eighty-eight civilian warriors would be on the way within minutes. He ended the call and walked back to the command center.

"Once Delta Foxtrot completes the mission, I'm officially on leave."

"Yes, Sir. Keep in touch."

"Will do."

"If you need us, we'll be there."

"Thanks soldier."

The Colonel returned the man's casual salute and turned on his heel feeling lighter than he had in a really long time.

————

"BANK LEFT."

"Roger banking left, target dead ahead."

"Movement. I have movement, three o'clock."

"Roger that."

"That's a civilian truck. I thought the area was abandoned, and this was just training."

"Call it up."

"Roger that. November-Golf, this is Delta Foxtrot lead."

"Go ahead, Delta."

"We have movement on target. Request instruction."

"Copy that, Delta. Do a flyover, and give me a minute."

"Roger."

The two aircraft raced high over the compound and the lead pilot looked down. Some of the buildings looked still intact, the fence was still up, but the truck was moving outside the blast zone. Not far enough away yet, but it was moving.

He was too high and fast to get a good look, but it was moving slowly. Strange.

"Bank right. Extend twenty clicks, execute left turn and return to target path," he instructed the pilot behind and slightly below him.

"Roger that."

This one would probably be aborted, until the area could be cleared of the civilian traffic, but at least they could buzz them and give them a thrill.

———

RAY LOOKED UP, smiling. He loved the look of those Air Force bombers. When they did exercises out here, his heart rose with patriotic pride. They sounded cool too, and he relished the boom as they flew over low and to his north. In his younger days he'd harbored ambitions of flying, but both his eyesight and his academics had squashed that dream.

So he'd done the only other thing he knew, and taken to farming and ranching. After the direction the country and the military had taken over the last couple of decades he was just as happy to have spent his career in the middle of nowhere Idaho.

Oh, sure, there were the typical nut jobs, building compounds and causing trouble. That was nothing new. Most of them were gone now anyway, chased back to Alabama or Oklahoma, somewhere down south anyway. Somewhere he didn't have to deal with them. Just up the gully stood one of their abandoned compounds, right under the flight path of those jets. He often wondered why they didn't just blow it up for target practice.

As he neared the left turn that headed to the compound, a

black SUV raced out of it, nearly colliding with his old Ford. The driver looked pale and crazed. The back window was down a little, and a mutt hung its head outside, panting, and barking at him and Travis Tritt as they sped by. In his rear-view mirror, he saw the SUV brake, and reverse. He slowed, and then stopped, wondering what the driver wanted, and if he needed help.

SPARKY BARKED from the back seat. *What is that old man doing out here?* I had to warn him.

Screeching to a halt, I shoved the SUV in reverse, intending to turn around. The old guy braked too, backing toward me in true rural Idaho fashion.

My leg was bleeding, and I really needed to get out of there, but the wound might scare him into complying.

With no time for formalities, I slid out of the driver's door, favoring my bad leg. "Howdy, friend," he said. "You need some help?" A mangy dog trotted up behind him.

"You gotta get out of here."

He saw the blood and shock spread over his face. "Looks like you need a doc." Sparky shot out of the driver's door, impatient, and landed on the packed dirt road.

He moved to the other dog, tail wagging, barking a quick hello, and took up tugging at the old man's sleeve. He sensed the need for urgency too.

"Not yet. No time to explain, but we gotta go."

The planes were gone for now, but they'd be back. His crawling truck was probably the only reason they didn't strike on the first pass.

"No, let me have a look at that," the old man said as he moved toward me.

"When those planes come back, they're gonna bomb that compound, and if they don't take out my truck too, I'm gonna be shocked. We gotta go. Climb in."

"They're looking for your truck, you say, right?"

"Yea."

"Then we take mine. My wife can help clean you up, then we'll figure out what's next. I just been down to the Sheriff's office, and I know something's up."

I looked around. He made sense. If they did take out the truck, they'd think they took me out too. I popped open the back.

"I gotta take a couple of things. You want to give me a hand?"

He grabbed the first bag I handed him, filled with C-4. He nearly dropped it. "What the hell is this?"

"I'll explain later. You want to help? This is helping."

Now he looked skeptical. "Look, I don't want to be involved in anything illegal."

"Trust me, I'm one of the good guys." I heard the distant drone of engines, and knew the planes had made their turn. It wouldn't be long now.

I didn't have time to wonder if I really was one of the good guys.

"I'll take your word for it, for now. But I wantcha to check in with the Sheriff once we get to my place."

"You bet. Now grab this one too."

He lugged two bags as I struggled with one, and we threw the large duffels into the back of his aging truck. The springs groaned, but didn't sag. Sparky and his dog both hopped up in the bed, and I limped to the passenger door, sliding in painfully.

He slammed his door a second later.

"Go fast," I instructed.

"Can do." He tipped his hat as the engine raced to life and he pressed the accelerator to the floor. The old truck rattled ahead. A valve ticking warned of future engine trouble, but other than that it sounded healthy. About half a mile down the road, he spotted the jets coming in, low and fast.

"Glorious ain't they?"

"When you're not the one they're after, yeah."

"You gonna share your story, friend?"

"Get us outta here, keep me alive, and we'll talk."

"Hell, that's easy." He pushed the accelerator harder, and the bed seemed like it might rattle off as we negotiated the back roads. "That's the secret to this washboard. Go faster, you hardly feel it. Kinda like flyin'."

I nodded, suddenly weak, and looked back. Both dogs stood feet apart, front paws on one of the bags, back paws on the metal bed, stable, but watching the sky to the rear.

"Good dog," I mumbled.

"Seems like it," he said.

Then I saw the bombers turn. If they were gonna drop, it should happen right about...

There.

————

"You sure that target's a decoy?"

"Yeah. Look, the rear gate is up, no one around now."

"What about the other truck we saw?"

"Gone. Concentrate and follow my lead."

"Roger that."

The target came up rapidly in his sights. Might as well use this chance to impress the brass with his skills. "Dropping in three, two, one."

The press of a button, count to three, then fly up and away.

"Get the truck?" He asked the pilot behind him.

"Got it."

"All right, let's turn for home."

They stayed relatively low. It was a short flight.

————

I saw the blast and shielded my eyes. "You can slow down now."

"You think we're out of the danger zone?"

"They're headed home. It'll take them a while to realize I'm not dead, if they do. It will buy us some time."

He slowed the truck a little. "Not long to my place now."

"Yeah. Hey thanks for stopping."

"I'm Ray, by the way."

"Pleased to meet you," I said, extending a hand painfully to shake. "I'm Todd, and that's Sparky back there."

He looked at me, and I saw a very perceptive man under the straw hat and western shirt. "When we get to my place, my wife'll fix you up. She used to be a nurse, and she's doctored plenty of men and animals out here on the ranch. We got a pretty good supply of what we need to patch a man. But I'll tell you, that looks like a gunshot wound. Just this morning, I picked up a soldier on this road, bloodied up too. Those bombers just blew the hell out of that compound you were runnin' from, and it appears to be at the center of this recent activity. The Sheriff says it's none of my concern, but now that I picked you up, I'm gonna make it my concern. So while she's fixing you up, you're gonna tell me your story."

"I can do that," I said, feeling tired, and willing to unload to anyone who would listen.

"You tell me the truth, and I'll decide what I'm gonna do with you, and who I call after that."

I nodded, staying quiet.

We neared the ranch, and another truck came down the road, headed the opposite direction. Its driver was the blackest man I'd seen in Idaho. He slowed and ran his window down. Ray followed suit.

"Let me do the talkin'," he said with a wink. "Hey Ray," the guy said, pulling alongside. "Hey Wayne."

"Didja see that explosion back there?"

"Yeah, some bombers out here playin'."

"Kinda cool. Who's this?"

"A new hand." Sparky wagged his tail in the back, and he and the other mutt barked in greeting. "That there's his dog."

"I didn't know you needed help."

"Just temporary. Where you headed all dressed up?"

"Gonna meet the new Governor. Big religious thing down in the capital, some big shot pastor that grew up here leading a rally. Chance of a lifetime. See history in the making."

"I'm a bit busy for all that, but you have a good time."

"Sure. Say hi to the missus for me."

"When's that rally?" I spoke up. But I already knew. It was the rally. The one I should have been working.

"Tomorrow night," he said.

I thought I knew what the Colonel might have in mind. Maybe even why he wanted me out of the picture. My hands got clammy with sweat, and I wasn't tired any more.

"Well, say hi to the Governor for us." I kept my voice as light as I could.

"Will do." He waved and pulled away.

"What the hell was that?" Ray asked.

"I just figured something out. Afraid we're in a hurry again."

He shook his head and pulled into the drive. As he did, Sparky and the mutt jumped down to join a small herd of other dogs prancing around the yard. Ray looked at them with an odd grin.

"Wonder where they all came from?"

A large woman came out to greet us, her face registering surprise at seeing me. It broke into a smile and Ray exited the vehicle rapidly, taking her in a quick embrace as I struggled from the other side of the truck.

His dog came over, wagged his tail and rubbed against me.

"That's Travis," he said, turning toward me as his wife disappeared back inside.

"Travis?" I tried not to get knocked off my feet.

"Yeah, like the Country singer. C'mon, let's get you inside."

I leaned on his shoulder as he guided me through the door. Travis quietly joined a circle of the previously unruly dogs.

Sparky whined and emitted quiet barks while they cocked their heads, focused on his every sound.

———

"ANDERSON."

"Delta-Foxtrot complete and code green, Sir."

"Thanks."

"Good luck, Sir. Have a good leave."

He hung up without answering. The soldier on the other end didn't know the whole truth of what he was doing, but he knew something big was going on.

It felt odd dressing in the uniform of the Cause for such a prestigious event. It was something he never would've done before. He couldn't be seen there in his military uniform, and perhaps he wouldn't put it on ever again.

With the last air strike, he had crossed a line, and he and his unit would likely be investigated, especially with fucking Malden snooping around. It was a risk and he hadn't come up with a cover story that would pass muster. After this little event, he might not care anymore. He'd be called back from leave pretty quickly, but he'd left the ruse that he'd be out fishing in the wilderness and unavailable. It would buy him some time, hopefully just enough.

He set his work phone down on the dresser, staring at it, moving to turn it off, but instead caressing the screen. Always tethered. Always available. It was time to cut the cord. Dropping it to the floor, he crushed it beneath the heel of his boot. From his pocket, another phone chirped. "Anderson."

"The first group has arrived. Do you want to brief them personally, Sir?"

"I'll be there in fifteen."

He shrugged on a light jacket and headed out the door, not bothering to lock it or set the alarm.

Today marked the beginning of a new time in his life, and it was time for him to take a big dose of Fuckitol.

Once in his car, he dialed another number.

"Arnold," the voice answered.

"Anderson here, how are you?"

"Good. Listen things are going well. Those tech stocks you tipped took off..."

"Yeah, great. Listen, you remember when we talked about the Zoo?"

"Yes, but—"

"Arnold, it's feeding time at the Zoo. Make it happen."

"Are you sure? You know what this means, right?"

"You'll be well compensated. I'll be in touch."

He ended the connection, shifted into gear and drove away, not looking back.

CHAPTER FOURTEEN

The skateboard went first, off the center of the rail. A critical moment, the boys nailed it. Dead center in the windshield. Next the body, only a second behind.

It struck, and the Mercedes screeched to a halt. Just as planned. Give him a minute...

Stunned, he made his way around the car. Anderson watched his mouth move as he spoke. Clarke had seen enough death, caused enough, he should know it well.

Out of the game for a while, the death he was used to was purposeful, not like this, not accidental.

Clarke sat down, heavily. Surely he wasn't injured, not too badly?

"Move in," he spoke into the radio, still watching through the scope.

The second car moved in, an amateur actor that was part of the Cause, and from Florida, flown in just for this job. No one would ever trace him, ever question him. He saw the approach, the feigned concern.

"Emergency units, now."

"Moving."

Sirens sounded. The other lanes were still empty, stacked behind a jack-knifed semi three miles down the road. A member pretended to be a new, incompetent tow truck operator, and would delay as long as he dared.

Deputies blocked the only other entrance between here and there. Sitting with sirens flashing, they raised no questions, at least for now.

Twenty minutes on that side, forty on the other. Then the accident and the subsequent cleanup would take care of itself, looking perfectly normal.

"Trooper," he said. This one was the trickiest.

"Present him with an imminent threat of death. The rest will take care of itself," he'd coached.

The trooper approached the boy. Genuine grief, that was good. The body did look like his son. A dead ringer, you could say.

He didn't even pull his weapon. Just ran at him like he'd strangle him. Must be the stress. Clarke defended himself well. The trooper would be in real pain.

The gun came out then, just as the second cruiser, still a member, but irrelevant, rolled on scene.

EMTs.

The fire truck, also filled with Cause guys.

Clarke fired, center mass. The trooper's body jerked as the slugs hit. They would leave bruises.

Clarke was tackled. Put in the back of the car. The trooper covered with a sheet. Taken away. The body awaited in the ambulance, ready to be dropped at the airport and airborne within the hour. The boy waited for him there.

All according to plan.

If Clarke had taken head shots, if he'd deviated at all from his training, all would have been lost. But he didn't. A true soldier's soldier.

Now, the good old American justice system would put him right where Colonel Anderson wanted him, and where he would be easy to eliminate without suspicion.

———

Marsha woke slowly.

Sight came first, a red outside her lids that told her there was bright light somewhere. Opening them a little at a time revealed little other than a tiny non- descript hotel room, eggshell white walls, and cheap furniture. It appeared she was alone on a large bed, fitted with comfortable, albeit cheap, linen. At least it smelled clean.

Another smell soon overwhelmed the fabric softener-scented blankets. Coffee. Not cheap like the linens either, but the scent of a deep, bold Columbian. The smell woke her stomach, and she heard it growl loudly.

The sound of a flushing toilet startled her, and she sat up, just realizing she wore pajama pants but no top. She jerked the sheet up to cover herself.

A large man walked calmly into the room and nodded to her. "So you're awake."

"Yes. Who are you?"

"A friend of your husband's. Just call me Wilson."

"Okay, Wilson. Where am I? What happened?"

"Let's just say I saved you in the nick of time. But that wouldn't be quite accurate. I was actually late."

"Late?"

"Yeah. A dog saved you. I didn't even know you guys owned a dog."

"We don't. Or didn't. Listen, forgive my lack of trust..."

"He was right about you. You have a birthmark, left ass cheek, just below where your jeans normally ride, shaped like a small heart. I've seen pictures."

"What?"

"That's what he told me to tell you, if we ever met. He told me this a long time ago. I think we both knew this day was coming, but we both hoped it wouldn't. That perhaps you and I would meet under better circumstances."

"So you served with him, before?"

"Yeah, before you."

"And?"

"Someone is after him. More than just bounty hunters. I know who, and I came to collect you last night, to protect you."

"Protect me?"

"It's a huge network. We don't know why the sudden interest now, but we'll figure that out. First priority, survival. Would you like some breakfast, Vivian?"

"Vivian? You must have the wrong person. My name is Marsha."

"Not for now. Here's your new ID. I'll give you some privacy to get dressed."

He set the card on a table at the end of the bed, and turned on the TV. "Watch while you get dressed, and I'll explain at Lenny's."

"Lenny's?"

"What better place for breakfast and a chat?"

Just then his phone rang. He glanced at it. "Gotta take this. Back in five. Be dressed and ready to go."

"Are we coming back to this room?"

"Nope."

"I need some things."

"We'll talk in a few. Dress." He pulled open the door and stepped into what had to be a hallway.

"Wilson," she heard him answer his phone, and then the door clicked shut.

Five minutes? Who was he kidding?

She picked up the new ID, barely looking at it other than to note that it was an Oregon driver's license, the name on it was indeed Vivian, and the address was in Ontario, Oregon. Interesting. Slipping from the bed and walking the short distance to the bathroom, she took off the thin pajama shorts. There was an outfit on a hanger, complete with underwear and bra. A pair of her favorite running sneakers sat on the floor. Locking the door, she stepped into the shower.

If he'd wait five minutes, he'd wait at least ten for her to get cleaned up.

Her eyes filled with tears as she thought of the stray dog and the strange events of the previous day.

Despite knowing there was no way the water would get hot enough to wash her cares away, she turned it up, determined to try.

———

BENJAMIN STOOD on the edge of the stage, looking out at the empty stadium. It was hard to believe that in this, the capitol city of a state once renowned for fanatical racism, this stadium would soon be filled with African Americans shouting praises to the Lord, and speaking of progressive, inclusive politics. He felt foolish for hiring the local security company to safeguard the event.

Shortly after, the incredible outpouring of support from the community brought him to tears. Hundreds had volunteered, white, black, Hispanic, and even Burmese. A local chapter of migrant workers provided fresh deli trays of locally grown produce to feed the security team and the event workers backstage. Local wineries and breweries agreed to supply drinks.

Glorious.

Praise be to the most high God.

He'd been in this stadium once, as a child, awed by the number of seats and the football players who looked like ants far below on the field. That same field now held a stage, set near the fifty-yard line, the famous turf covered by temporary tiles.

His foster parents had done the best they could to raise him, and applauded his decision to attend seminary, offering all of the support they could. But he'd always struggled, a minority in a part of the country still dominated by white males. He'd been harassed at school, on the playground, on the way home. An athlete, the only thing that made school bearable was his aptitude for sports. There were classmates who resented him, sure. But it had kept him sane, and he took hope daily from the words of Martin Luther King and other champions of the equality movement.

Now the first African American Governor of the state would stand with him here, the dreams of his youth realized.

"Penny for your thoughts."

"Annabelle, don't sneak up on an old man like that."

"You'll never be old to me."

He pulled her tiny frame into his bear-like embrace, folding himself around her smaller form.

"I love you."

"I love you too."

"I'm proud of you, Benjamin."

"That means more to me than all of this."

"Then I must tell you so every day."

They both faced the empty seats in silence, holding hands.

"Are you ready?" she asked.

"No. And yes. Can I give you my speech again?"

"Certainly." She rose on her toes to kiss his cheek, and they turned to go backstage. "What's happening here today..."

"It's a miracle. I know."

"It's tomorrow's history."

"I've wanted to be a part of this for so long."

She glanced at her watch, and he watched her hands, her delicate movements, the strength of her femininity that had drawn him to her in the first place, in a college class on another campus not so far from here. "Less than twenty-four hours now." Her smile warmed his heart.

As she followed him off the stage, he noticed some setup and security people enter through the north end zone entrance. Behind them, a cart followed filled with hundreds of folding chairs.

———

"GENERAL MALDEN HERE."

"He did what? Jesus Christ! Where is he?"

"What do you mean, leave? What do you mean you couldn't stop him?"

"I'm in Denver now. I'll be there in two hours. When I land, I want some answers. And you find Anderson and have his ass waiting for me. I don't care if you have to issue a fucking arrest warrant and put out an APB."

"Yes, I know what's going on tomorrow. I know your security is stretched thin. I just don't give a shit. I want his ass, and I want it now."

He ended the connection. Malden had always known Anderson was a bit out there, on the edge of Section 8, but something more sinister was going on. The guys in his unit weren't even sharing where he'd gone, if they knew. But they were hiding something, and he would discover what it was, one way or another.

The military system would take a long time to coordinate an investigation into a full bird Colonel, and he knew he couldn't hold him for long without a valid reason.

Malden had served a long time, overseas and even at Gitmo in the bad old days. There were plenty of unofficial ways to get answers.

———

"Colonel."

He almost returned the military salute instead of the one more appropriate here. Stopping himself, he responded with the salute of the Brethren. "Where are you from?" he asked the Sergeant.

"Wyoming. There are only six of us, but it's a small state."

"That's fine. You have a small chapter. You made good time."

"Yes, Sir. One of our men is a pilot."

"Excellent. That your dog over there?" He gestured at a reddish-haired, medium- sized pup sniffing around the door that led outside.

"Yeah, she goes everywhere with me."

"What kind is she?"

"No one knows. Just a mutt."

"She doesn't mind flying?"

"Nope. Don't bother her a bit."

"Huh. Well, carry on. Get your men checked in. Once the others get here, I'll brief all of you. Tomorrow will be a glorious night."

The new arrival snapped his heels together and saluted again. "Long live the Cause, Sir. It's an honor."

As he walked away, the Colonel's phone beeped. "Anderson."

"You need to lay low, Sir."

"Why?"

"Malden is coming, and with a hard on for you. He'll be here in two hours, and ordered that you be found and brought in."

"What did you tell him?"

"I didn't talk to him. He suspects something is going on with the unit and won't talk to us."

"The air strike?"

"He's pissed, Sir. What do you want me to tell him when he asks?"

"Tell him it was an urgent matter of national security, and that's all I'd tell you. I'll deal with the rest when I get back."

"Will you be coming back?"

"Not until after tonight. I'll let you know."

"Yes, Sir. I'll do my best. Good luck."

"You too."

Fucking Malden. He didn't have time though. No matter how good he was, and how quick he found anything out, he didn't have time to fix this one. Only someone operating outside the system who had some idea what he might be doing could stop Operation Charlie now. The only person who knew enough was dead, finally. Consequences be damned.

He wasn't going back anyway. After this, his career was over.

———

"JESUS CLARKE, WHERE HAVE YOU BEEN?"

"Getting doctored up at a ranch in the middle of nowhere."

"What?"

"I'll explain when I can. I'm headed out soon."

"Okay, let me know where you want to meet. I have hardware, and I have Marsha."

"Good. I'll contact you again soon."

I ended the call and looked at Alma. "You held still very well last night Todd."

"It's not my first time being shot."

"I don't imagine so. Did you sleep well?"

I shrugged. "Well enough."

"Are you sure we don't know each other? You look awful familiar."

She busied herself with coffee and breakfast, and my stomach growled. Sparky lay at my feet, Travis beside him. Both dogs looked up expectantly, hoping for scraps.

"Yeah, he does." Ray walked in, carrying a printed piece of paper. He saw my glance. "Ranchers use computers too. A military career in—" he looked through the glasses on the end of his nose and read carefully from the sheet he held "—special forces including covert operations in several foreign countries make this man a dangerous fugitive. He should be considered armed and dangerous."

Alma stopped stirring.

"Don't jump to conclusions, Ray." I held up my hand in my defense.

"You killed a cop, it says here."

He had a gun in his hand, and I sighed. "Yeah, I did." I looked down at the table. The horrible memory flooded back.

"Says here it was self-defense, but you skipped bail. Want to tell me about that?" I heard the rustle of clothing as he took a seat across from me. The gun lay on the table between us.

The warrior told me to take it. *Shoot them. Escape.* I didn't have time for this conversation right now. I didn't have time to explain. My hand flexed under the table. They wouldn't be the first.

Kill. Kill. Kill, and move on.

Fur slid under my hand, and the warrior quieted. Sparky pushed his way in to be petted.

"I didn't mean to. And something else is going on here. I've had an army after me. Not just bounty hunters. It's about more than just me jumping bail."

"Why?" He looked calmly at me and I was no longer sure I could take the gun from him.

"I used to be a spy."

"So?"

"Kind of like internal affairs. An inside spy."

"You ratted on someone."

"More than one."

"For what?"

"White supremacist tendencies. Using military power to stack a unit with sympathizers."

"What happened?"

"Nothing. The report went nowhere. I was captured." I stopped, deciding how far to go. "I was tortured. Threatened. Injured, quietly discharged, and told to keep quiet."

"And now?"

"I don't know about the timing, but for some reason they suddenly want me out of the way."

"You suspect something."

"The rally tonight. The guy I was investigating, Colonel Anderson. He's the only one who could throw this much at me."

"The rally?"

"The one your friend mentioned for the new governor? The first African American Governor in the state? And the guy leading it? That Reverend Wolfe or whatever he calls himself? Anderson hates him."

"So you want me to let you walk out of here? Not call anybody?"

"Not exactly. I need your phone, and maybe to use your computer. I may need to borrow your truck."

"What?"

I looked down at my leg and nodded to his wife. "Thanks for patching me up. I'm sorry."

I grabbed the gun from the table before he could react and pointed it at him. "Afraid I might not have time to ask nicely."

From the floor, Travis growled at me, deep in his throat. Sparky moved between us, and they stood growling at each other.

My leg exploded in pain. Ray jumped at me, and the barking and snarling of a dog fight began.

Ray grabbed at my gun hand, and I didn't want to. I tried not to, but my vision turned crimson.

A second later, I heard a gunshot echo as if from far, far away. A woman screamed and a dog howled in pain and sorrow.

———

"Colonel Anderson, please."

"He's out on leave."

"When will he return?"

"May I ask who's calling?"

"This is Bobbie Ann Sullivan. I'm a reporter, and I have some questions for him regarding some recent events here in Idaho."

"I'm sorry, ma'am. I don't know when he'll return. Would you like to leave your number?"

"Is there anyone else who can comment on recent military activity in the area of—"

"No ma'am. Would you like the number of the public relations department?"

"No thanks. I already have it. Thanks for your time."

Fourth message. What the hell is going on here? she thought. *The military is conducting some kind of operation inside our borders, in this state, and no one knows a thing?* If the Sheriff is right, there are dead bodies, civilian and military, somewhere.

A cover up? Of what?

"Sheriff?"

"Yeah, Bobbie?" He poked his head around the door of the office he'd let her use.

"I got nothing here. No one's talking. Can we go out to that compound?"

"Sure, but I don't know why. We won't be able to get in."

"I just want to look around, that's all."

For a moment, she wasn't sure he'd say yes, but finally he nodded. Good, she didn't relish going by herself, although she would've.

As they walked out the door, she noticed an unfamiliar mutt without a collar watching from across the street, sitting perfectly still.

Odd.

As her eyes met the dog's, it shook its head, scratched at an ear with its hind paw, and then turned to trot away, stopping only to urinate on a nearby fire hydrant.

———

DALE SAW SMOKE AHEAD, coming from the direction of that fucking compound. Coming from the compound itself, he'd bet.

He was sick of fucking waiting. Men were dead, his friends. He'd had no word from that Colonel. And now his dog had run off, and not come back. That had been the last straw. Seemed stupid, but he loved that dog like a kid. Time to go find him. No more fucking around.

There were dogs everywhere lately. He knew they were common in this area and owning more than one seemed to be the norm. So was letting them run loose. Usually they stuck close to home. He'd seen three strays so far out on this quiet road.

He drove on, the smell of smoke growing stronger the further he went. He looked at the pistol lying on the center of the seat. The rifle in the gun rack. It would be enough if he ran into trouble.

Really? You expect to run into trouble? Yeah, I kinda do. And I almost hope I do.

Just before the turnoff he spotted a burned-out SUV. Looked like the one parked inside the fence when they'd made their assault. Maybe somebody got the guy. Just too bad it hadn't been him.

He gripped the wheel, making the turn north. The smoke subsided a little bit, but it was dead ahead now. Less than a quarter mile in, he had to stop. Scorched black earth surrounded the road, and some of the trees still smoldered. A small crater made the road impassable.

Stepping out with the pistol in his right hand, he surveyed the scene, the acrid scent of gunpowder assaulting his nostrils. The silence was eerie. Leaving the road, he spotted a strange lump on the still warm ground ahead. In a few rapid steps he could see it was a body.

Still gripping a rifle, the soldier's clothing had been burned away. He felt bile rise in the back of his throat and suppressed a gag. That's when he noticed the sickly- sweet smell of burned flesh. He flashed back to his time in Iraq, the smell reminiscent of the one they'd come across on the scene of a rocket attack. The bodies there had still been standing, burned in place, held fast by the sands of the desert turned to glass by the heat.

The ground was littered from here to the gate with at least a dozen fried lumps. He walked forward, studying each one, resisting the urge to roll them over, to check for the life he knew was no longer there.

Near the fence he could see the buildings of the compound were gone save for a few skeletal walls. At least five large craters circled the interior of the fence. Some of the debris still smoldered, some of the piles still held slowly dying fires. The fence itself was warped outward, as if pushed by a giant hand. Some of the supports were bent, bowed in quiet supplication. He approached it with renewed caution, knowing the metal would blister any skin that touched it. Right next to the fence was a smaller lump, and his throat closed when he saw it.

No, it couldn't be. Not possible. Please God, no.

The dog's head was a mess, at least half gone from a gunshot. A red collar decorated its neck.

The same color as Ricky's.

He knelt down. The tag was still intact. Touching it, he needed to see, didn't want to see.

It burned his reaching fingers. Setting the gun on the ground, he wrapped his hand with the tail of his shirt, reaching out again.

He turned it toward him, knowing already what it said. Ricky.

The charred body was all that remained of his constant companion, his best friend. Tears began to leak from the corners of his eyes. As his hand reached out to feel the ashen fur, he heard a voice from behind.

"Leave the gun on the ground. Hands up. Stand up nice and slow for me. No sudden moves, and it'll all be okay."

Held his hands up the best he could, his sobs becoming audible, his shoulders shaking with grief, and struggled to his feet.

CHAPTER FIFTEEN

"You okay?"

"Yeah, where's my son?"

"He'll be here soon."

"You sure that wasn't him? It looked like him. I lost it there for a minute."

Colonel Anderson almost smiled at the grimace on the man's face as he removed the vest, now stained with the fake blood packets that had burst on impact. He didn't know how they did it, but he loved special effects.

"He's safe, I assure you."

"I need more than just your assurance."

"Half hour. You're airborne and out of the country."

"Listen you prick, he better be all right."

"He is. In fact, here he comes now."

Tyler limped out from behind the building, and ran into his father's arms. They talked for a moment, and he gave them some privacy. It was the best he could do.

Their escort nodded at the Colonel, and he nodded back.

"Gentlemen, I have to go," he said quietly. "Thank you for your service, and your dedication to the Cause."

"You're welcome." Tears welled in the father's eyes as he clutched his

151

boy to himself. For a moment, Anderson almost felt sorry for them. Almost.

The three exchanged a salute he was sure the boy did not understand fully. The jet engines roared to life, and he watched as the plane left the hangar. It was a shame he would never see the two of them again.

———

SHE SEWED QUIETLY, and although I knew she was no longer a threat, I still held the gun on the pair. Sparky sat quietly at my left side, staring straight ahead.

Their dog, Travis, lay at her feet. He panted, clearly in pain, but not injured too badly. Scratches on his snout and a shallow bite mark on his shoulder were the only visible evidence of injury, other than his eyes. His goddamn pain-filled eyes.

Until I met Sparky, I never knew a dog's eyes could be so expressive, their faces so easy to read. I'd pretty much ignored dogs for the better part of my life. Now for about the hundredth time in a couple of days, a dog had saved my life, and I'd saved theirs too.

Travis' eyes asked me, "Why?" Sparky's first glance asked me, "Why?"

When Alma finished screaming, she asked me, "Why?"

I'm a warrior, that's why.

I couldn't tell them that. Couldn't say pure ingrained instinct from years of training caused me to kill the cop, and to shoot Ray.

A pretty nice guy who tried to help me out and keep his wife safe.

At least you just winged him, the warrior declared. *It could have been worse. Much worse.*

Sparky whined at that.

Ray's wife kept stitching his shoulder, just as she'd done my leg.

Which still ached like hell where she'd stabbed the needle in when I'd grabbed the gun.

Ray stared at me, rage smoldering in his eyes. I understood completely.

"What next, big guy?" he asked. Good question. First thing I needed—his phone. There was a handset in a charger on the table behind me. I stepped back slowly, grabbed it, and punched in memorized numbers.

"Wilson."

"Wilson, I've encountered a delay."

"Shit. What now?"

"I had to take care of some friends. I know what Anderson is planning."

"Yeah?"

"Yeah. And he thinks I'm dead."

"You want to share?"

"He had the compound bombed. The rally in Boise tonight—"

"Yeah, I know, the new Governor and that Ben dude, the one that heads that big church."

"Anderson hates them both."

"How much pull do you think he has, Clarke?"

I hesitated. He'd been crossing lines for at least the last few days chasing me. "He has to have aroused suspicion in someone. But there's always the members of The Cause."

"What do they have?"

"In the state, not much, but if he brings in outside groups? Depends on how long he's been planning. As far as armament? The feds never seized all the weapons they had. So I have no idea. It could be extensive."

"Security for the event will be tight, though, right?"

"Very. But it's always possible he has someone on the inside. Probably more than one someone."

"Okay, so what do you want me to do?"

"Meet me at the shopping center near 55 in..." I looked at my captives. Done sewing, Alma worked on mopping up the spilled blood with an already soaked towel. I grabbed a fresh one from the floor and tossed it to her. She nodded, although I'm not sure it was in gratitude. "In three hours. How's Marsha?"

"Okay, I guess."

"Just keep her away from this."

"What exactly are you planning to do?"

"I have no idea."

"So what do you want me to bring?"

"Everything."

"Will do."

I hung up and looked at Ray, Alma, and Travis. Sparky joined him, and licked his wounds. They acted like old friends.

"I'm sorry to ask after all...this. But I need your help."

Ray shook his head. Alma put a hand on his shoulder. "Hear him out."

He moved to fold his arms, then winced, realizing he couldn't with his injured shoulder. "I'm listening."

In his eyes, the anger still smoldered, but I couldn't do a thing about it. The time was short.

———

"What are you doing here, Dale?"

He held Ricky's collar in his hands, the only thing he'd been able to bring himself to take from his dog. They were cuffed together, and he sat on the road near the gate. The gravel of the road bit into his ass even through his thick jeans, but he didn't care. Despite the human carnage that surrounded him, every time the thought of his poor dog entered his head, he began to sob just a little. The Sheriff's question ignited a spark of anger.

"I wanted some goddamn answers. I was hired to collect a bounty, apparently on a military mad man, and my men, some of them friends, died. My dog saved my life, damn near turned on me and disappeared, and I was told the whole thing was classified by some prick Colonel, and now you just want me to go home and pretend nothing happened?"

"No Dale, but there are channels—"

"What are you doing here, Sheriff?"

He looked over at Bobbie Ann. "She insisted that we at least drive up here. Truth be told, I want the same answers you do. I don't like the military operating in my back-yard chasing what at first appears to be a bail jumper, and then bringing World War Three down on our heads."

"So how come I'm wearing cuffs?"

"I needed to make sure you have nothing to do with this."

"We don't know each other well, but you're ex-military right?" Dale asked.

"Yeah." They both watched as Bobbie Ann walked around, snapping pictures with a pocket camera and taking notes.

"We took two different paths. Me, I went into business for myself, entering the private trade of chasing down the bad guys. Why? Hell, I don't know. Maybe I had enough of the military life and didn't want to join a civilian para-military organization, like a police force. Maybe I don't trust my government and didn't want to work with them anymore. Maybe this kind of thing is why. I saw too many black ops where guys like these disappeared for no reason."

"I hear you. It hasn't been easy to stick with law enforcement, even long enough to become Sheriff and keep the office in a small county. I almost quit, more than once."

Dale nodded. "You got a smoke?"

"Nope, I quit."

"Too bad. Good men I brought with me are dead. My best friend is dead." He looked down at the collar, fighting tears. "And for what? Or rather who? Why is this Clarke so important? Is he this important?" He gestured around. "You see why I needed answers? You see why I came?"

Kneeling, the uniform-clad man undid the cuffs. "Yeah, I do. Maybe we can find some together. Maybe she can help."

They both looked for the reporter, but she wasn't anywhere in sight.

"Where'd she go?" Dale asked.

"Bobbie Ann!" The Sheriff's voice echoed off the trees.

"Yeah?" came back faintly.

"Time to go. Get back over here."

"On the way," they both heard.

They turned and walked back to the hole in the road both vehicles sat beside. Dale stared at the collar in his hands, glancing around at the devastation. It couldn't be because of one guy. There had to be more to it.

Movement caught his eye. He looked to see Bobbie Ann moving slowly their way. She continued to snap pictures and stare in all directions. As she took her next step, Dale heard a loud click.

"Stop!" he yelled.

She froze, about twenty yards away. "Don't move! Did you hear that, Sheriff?"

He didn't need to ask. The officer stood, gun drawn, looking around. "I think you can put that away. I'll go check this out."

He nodded, but didn't put it away, instead staying ready, alert. "Ma'am, don't move!"

"I think I stepped on something." She sounded panicked.

"Probably. Just hold still. Don't shift your weight until I can check it out, okay?"

"Easy for you to say."

"Which foot?"

"My left."

"Okay." He edged forward, looking for signs of disturbed earth or fresh holes, but the task proved impossible. All of the ground was disturbed, charred, ripped with bullets or debris from a gun battle and a bombing. It was amazing that whatever she'd stepped on hadn't already blown.

If it was still active. If it was anything at all.

The click had sounded mechanical, not like a breaking twig, or two rocks sliding together.

He couldn't be sure. Not without looking.

Closing the distance, weighing every step, moving carefully, he made it ten yards. Halfway.

Boot tracks decorated the ground. Several men had walked right by this spot, and not one had stepped on...whatever it was.

As he slid forward, he heard another sound and looked up. Between him and the reporter stood a dog.

A mutt. A true Heinz 57, origins lost in a multi-branched family tree, there was no discerning his parentage or breed. He stood, front paws apart and braced, clearly aggressive.

"Easy boy," he cooed. "Easy."

A deep growl escaped the dog's throat, and he briefly saw the white flash of teeth. "Good boy. I'm not going to hurt you." He took another step, and the growling intensified. Teeth flashed in an expression far from a grin. Lifting his foot again elicited a fierce bark. From behind he heard a more familiar click.

"Sheriff, no!" He held up his hand and looked back. The officer's face was set in a grimace, squinting in concentration, his revolver pointed at the dog.

He heard a female whimper and turned back. Bobbie Ann stood still but weaving unsteadily as if she might pass out. On either side of her stood two Doberman mixes quietly staring at him. The first dog blocked Dale's progress, but now he sat, simply guarding the path.

In his peripheral vision he saw at least a dozen dogs appear from the woods around them. Another dozen materialized behind the scowling Sheriff.

They were surrounded.

———

"ONE HOUR. That's all the time you have." Ray told him.

"Thank you."

"Don't thank me. I owe you a gunshot wound. If it turns out you're wrong, I'll make sure you hang."

"Clarke?"

"Yes ma'am?"

"I'm sorry about all this. Will your leg be okay?"

Ray glared at his wife, but she ignored him.

"Yes ma'am. It will have to be. For what it's worth Ray, I'm sorry I shot you. I'm sorry to have troubled you both."

"I want my truck back when you're done."

"Yes, Sir."

Sparky barked, reminding me that we had to be on our way.

I walked out the door jingling his keys in my hand. Sparky hopped up in the passenger seat like he belonged there. Under other circumstances, it might have been comical. I'd never known how comforting it was to have a dog, and no matter what happened afterwards, I knew I'd always own one.

Headed down the road, I pushed the truck as fast as I dared. If I planned to meet Wilson in Boise on time, I needed to hurry.

We neared the turnoff for the compound, and through the trees I saw what appeared to be two vehicles in the driveway, not far in.

Shit.

Sparky barked, and I looked at him. Another bark, one sharp sound told me he wanted me to stop.

I looked ahead, and two dogs stood in the center of the road. Slamming on the brakes, the truck skidded to a stop. I had no choice but to negotiate the turn, and we pulled up behind a Sheriff's cruiser and a black pickup.

The Sheriff turned as we arrived. He held a revolver, cocked, but pointed at the ground. About ten yards away another man stood very still. Directly in front of him a mutt sat between him and a woman standing, pale and frightened, flanked by the two now familiar Dobermman mixes. I glanced around and noticed we were surrounded by dogs. I shut off the truck and got out.

The Sheriff started to raise his weapon, and a chorus of

growls rose around us. Sparky sprinted out to put himself between me and the officer.

"Lay it down, nice and slow." I pointed my own weapon at him, and he complied with a frown.

The other man turned. "Hey, you're ..."

"Yeah. What's going on here?" I asked, thinking I already knew.

"She stepped on something." He pointed to the woman.

"I figured that."

"Can you call off these dogs, so I can get to her?" Sparky looked expectantly up at me.

"Stay." I told the Sheriff. Walking over, I scanned for more traps, hardly believing this one hadn't been set off by the bombs they'd dropped on the area. Sparky stayed at my side.

"Are you who I think you are?" the Sheriff asked.

"Can we talk a little later, sir?" I answered, not looking at him. "Your lady friend there is in a bit of a bind."

"You're going to help her out?"

"I am."

"You killed all these men?"

"Not exactly, Sir. I defended myself, yes."

"And my dog?" the first man asked.

"I didn't kill any dogs. I'll explain later. Shut up, gentlemen." I didn't want to be impatient, but the woman looked like she might faint. I knew I'd be vulnerable when I deactivated the pressure mine she'd stepped on, but the dogs would cover me.

I knelt down next to her, and saw her leg was shaking, the muscles tense. "What's your name ma'am?"

"Bobbie Ann."

"Hi Bobbie Ann. I'm Todd. I'm going to get you off this thing before you know it, but you need to relax and hold still for another couple minutes. Can you do that?"

"You sure you know what you're doing?"

"I set it. I know I can turn it off."

"Hurry please. My leg is really tired."

"Yeah, sorry about this." I apologized, something I'd been doing a lot of lately. Using my hands, I uncovered the side of the device and flicked the catches off a small panel. I unclipped a yellow wire, then a red. A small light went out.

"You can step away now."

She took a shaky step and fell to the ground in a dead faint.

Sparky barked and bared his teeth. A chorus of growls joined his. I turned and saw the Sheriff with his weapon pointed at my chest, closer than before.

"You're under arrest, Mr. Clarke."

The dogs closed in from behind, and the other man was forced to move to his side. Together they advanced.

"Sheriff. I need to explain, and there isn't much time." I had no time for this.

Kill, the warrior said. *Kill and move on. We have to go.*

Sparky's head slid under my hand. He raised it, forcing my fingers into his fur. His low growl radiated through his skull into my bones. The warrior quieted.

They stopped. The other man took a step back. Several of the dogs made a half circle behind me, closing in. Behind the two men another dozen completed the circle.

I didn't understand it, I didn't understand how Sparky communicated with them or why he, and therefore they, had chosen me. I simply accepted it. They were on my side.

"A bad guy is behind all this. I defended myself, and maybe I did some things wrong along the way. I'm happy to answer for that when the time comes. But these dogs, they defended me too. I'm not sure why I'm so special, except I think I might know what's happening next, and I'm pretty damn familiar with the guy's methods.

"If I'm right, bad stuff will happen tonight. If I'm going to even try to stop it, I have to get moving. Believe me or not, with or without your cooperation, I have to go."

"I'll shoot."

"If you get that shot off, it might be the last thing you do." I looked meaningfully at the dogs. My leg ached from standing still, and something in the back of my mind told me to *go, go, go.*

I needed to run.

Time flew faster and faster.

"Give me a name. Who's behind this?"

"Colonel Mike Anderson."

Both men looked at each other, and the Sheriff lowered his weapon. "Talk fast."

The woman sat up, bleeding from a small cut on her head. "What's going on?" she asked.

"Your friend here is about to tell us a story."

She raised a small camera and snapped my picture. I blinked in surprise. Rolling a little to her right, she pulled a notebook and a broken pen from her back pocket. Cursing, she asked, "One of you fellas have something I can write with?"

Pulling a pen from my pocket, I tossed it to her. "You a reporter?"

"Yeah."

"Good. You're riding with me, at least for now. I think it's time for some introductions and then I'll make this quick." As I relaxed, so did the dogs, widening the circle, but remaining watchful.

CHAPTER SIXTEEN

"It's hot here, Dad." Tyler complained.

"I know, kiddo. What did you expect? It's Mexico."

"Are we going to stay here?"

"No."

"Where are we going?"

"Somewhere in South America I think."

"Why did we have to do this?"

"For the good of the Cause."

"Will we ever be able to go back?"

"I hope so."

"I need to call my friends." Tyler crossed his arms, defiant.

"Not yet."

"I told them I would."

"They'll have to wait."

A knock sounded at the door of the hotel room. He wasn't expecting anyone.

"Who is it?"

"Policia. Abrir la puerta."

"Ingles?" he replied, looking around, wondering why they could be here.

"Open the door Senor," came the answer.

"Just a moment." He shot Tyler a look. "Keep quiet kid, let me do the talking."

He opened the door, and two armed men shoved him aside. They made straight for his and his son's luggage. Ripping it open, they rifled through it.

"What are you looking for?"

"Las drugas." The statement was followed by a chuckle. "Aha!"

The officer turned around, and in his hand was a bag of white powder Tyler's father had never seen before.

"That's not mine."

"Sure senor. I have never heard that one before." The police officer laughed.

A second later his partner straightened from his search of Tyler's bag. He too stood up with a chuckle of triumph, holding another bag. They laid them both on the table.

A pistol appeared. "Hands up!" The second soldier ordered roughly in heavily accented English.

"But—"

"Manos!" He brandished the pistol angrily.

The first officer carefully opened one bag, dipping his finger in the powder and tasting it. "Cocaine," he said simply.

A second later the former trooper found himself in handcuffs. Goddamn Mexico. He should've known better than to agree to this stopover.

A half an hour later he found himself alone in a barren cell. He had no idea where they'd taken Tyler.

A man entered. "Dinero?" He inquired. He shook his head no.

"Lo siento." A small pistol appeared in his hand, and he fired twice. The world disappeared.

———

"CAN I HELP YOU, KID?"

"Yeah, I want this board." Tommy told him.

"Sure man. That's a nice choice. Want me to ring you up?"

"I don't have the money quite yet."

"How much you got?"

"A hundred." Tommy answered, looking at the price tag.

"We got a nice one over here for seventy."

"I know. I don't want that one."

"Well, that one is one-sixty."

"I know. I should have it soon. Someone owes me money."

"Well, I hope for your sake it's still here when you get paid. These sell fast."

"Can't you like, take payments? Hold it for me or somethin' until I can come back. I'll give you the hundred down." Tommy was beyond desperate and tired of waiting.

"Listen, I'd love to kid. But I just work here. The owner would never go for it."

"He'll never have to know. Just the two of us. C'mon, hook me up."

"Sorry kid."

Tommy picked up the board, running his hand over it. It was hand painted. He spun the front wheels. Red Bones, smooth as silk. He didn't want to wait, not at all. He grabbed it at one end, making a decision. After all, he was already a criminal, right?

"Thanks anyway," he said, pretending to set the board down. The salesman reached out to pick it up, and Tommy swung it with all he had, striking him in the face.

"Wha—" Blood spurted from the man's broken nose. For a minute he felt bad, but he swung the board a second time, impacting the man's temple with a dull thud, and he fell to the floor, moaning.

Tommy sprinted for the door, weaving past a display at the front containing helmets and knee pads. Slamming the door open, he reached the sidewalk. A yell followed him out the door.

"Stopth himpth!" The words were distorted by a mangled face, but understandable. The few people on the street stared at him.

For a moment he froze, looking down at himself. The end of

the board he'd beaten the salesman with was bloody, and there were drops of blood on his shirt and the toes of his sneakers. He had to get out of here, so put the board down, and started to ride for all he was worth. A whistle sounded from behind him. "Stop!" a voice of authority commanded.

Pushing faster, jumping the curb and crossing against the light, he glanced behind, and saw a bicycle cop coming up fast.

Tommy had nowhere to go. Jumping the next curb, he headed for a long set of stairs that led down a hill to the green belt. Grinding halfway down, he knew he didn't have enough speed.

The cop was good. Bunny-hopping the first few steps, he stood on his pedals, riding down.

Tommy knew he was caught. As the board slowed, he jumped lightly off the rail, stopping on the steps. The cop halted his bike with a clever spin and the application of both brakes. Dropping it, he faced Tommy.

"You know the drill?"

"Yeah." He raised his hands and turned around. "Nice grind," the cop said as he cuffed him. "Thanks. Nice riding."

"You took that board?"

"Yeah man. Sorry."

"Too bad. Over a hundred bucks, I'd say. Makes that a misde-meanor. You been in trouble before?"

"Not like this."

"Why do you look familiar?"

"I testified as a witness in a case not long ago."

"Oh yeah?"

"Yeah. What if I had some information related to that case that someone might find interesting?"

"Like what?"

"Like maybe I haven't been paid for the stuff I said at that trial, and maybe it wasn't all exactly true."

"What are you saying, son?"

"There was a guy there, Mr. Jeffers?"

"Yeah, the prosecutor. I know him."

"I want to talk to him."

"Listen, kid, I'm just a cop, but you might want a lawyer before you do something like that."

"I'm just fine."

"I have to read you your rights, but I'll make a call for you when we get to the station."

Tommy stayed quiet. If Tyler had called, if he'd gotten the damn money when he was supposed to, he wouldn't be in this situation. So fuck him, and fuck the deal.

He was going to save his own ass, the rest of them be damned. They could call him a rat from jail for all he cared.

Tommy watched with some relief as a patrol car pulled up on the street above, and the cop walked him back up the stairs. He looked back with longing at the board. Maybe he would be able to actually buy it when all of this trouble was over.

———

"I'm going, Wilson." Marsha said.

"No, actually you aren't."

"I have to see him."

"He told me to keep you out of this. You want to go, you go on your own."

"But—"

"Listen Marsha, I like you, but my loyalty is to Todd. I'm not going against what he said, and that's final."

He closed the door and walked out. She watched through the blinds as he closed the back of the SUV and got into the driver's seat. Earlier, he'd loaded bags of God knew what kind of military hardware. Admittedly, he was going to face an uncertain threat. Todd was out there, operating on military instincts that might or might not be out of date against an adversary with all kinds of resources.

Fulfilling her threat, she'd sent the letters. If the Colonel resurfaced, he'd be ruined. It might not even matter after tomorrow, but it might. Marsha wanted to know.

Also, she missed Todd terribly. When they'd got married, he'd assured her all of this was over. There would be no more military, no more secret trips and being gone who knew where doing who knew what. The accident, his arrest, the *in-absentia* trial, and his running had all changed that. She just wanted things to be like they were before, and on every level that mattered, she knew they never would be.

She'd known the warrior side existed in him somewhere, but never expected it to come out and show up like this.

Marsha wanted, no, needed to go to him, and Wilson hadn't even shared where he was headed.

A second later, an insistent scratching started at the front door. Unable to see anything from the window, she went to investigate. It started again, sounding just like the dog from the other night. Her eyes welled with tears at the memory. The whole time she'd been staying here with Wilson she hadn't seen a single dog around at all, not even on a walk with its owner.

Outside the door, sat a near-duplicate of the dog that had saved her life. The tears now spilled from her eyes, but she wiped them roughly away. Tail wagging, the dog started forward, then sat expectantly. Started forward again, and settled back as if saying, "Hey, is it okay if I come inside?"

Wiping her running nose, she stifled a giggle. "Sure, come on in."

The dog barked and wagged its way past her. She knelt, petting its head and scratching behind its ears. "Good dog. What are you doing here?"

As if in answer the dog ran for the kitchen, and she followed. Her purse hung on the back of a chair, and the dog pulled it down.

"Whoa! You drop that." The dog obeyed, but the purse opened a little when it struck the floor. The black nose darted inside. "Hey!" she said, lunging forward.

The dog held her car keys in its mouth. It was still in the garage at her house a few miles away.

"What?" she asked the dog.

The pooch walked over and dropped the keys at her feet. Kneeling to retrieve them, she was greeted with a hearty bark. The dog seemed...intelligent. Just like the dog before. Studying it closely, she picked up the keys. No, not the dog from before, but certainly a close relative. A brother from the same litter, a cousin perhaps, if dogs had that kind of thing.

"You want to go for a ride?"

The dog barked and spun in a circle, then sat, looking anxiously at her. "My car's not here."

A bark and a tail wag in return.

Go get it, he seemed to say.

An old TV show popped into her head. Lassie, where a Collie was always pulling Timmy or one of his friends out of a jam. It always seemed so unrealistic to her when the dog would bark, and his parents would respond with something ridiculous, like "What's that girl? Timmy's down the well?"

This felt like that, but real life. The dog's thoughts were written on its face, expressing what it would say if it could talk. It felt, well, it felt insane, yet somehow it felt right too.

"You want to find Todd?" she asked. Another bark and a circle.

A crazy idea entered her head. Wilson was headed to some rendezvous point, and Boise was huge. Still, she had a feeling maybe the dog could help lead her to him, like some kind of bloodhound.

She grabbed her cell and called for a cab.

———

Making the call seemed insane to Sherriff Crawford, but he made it anyway. Todd's argument was compelling. "How may I direct your call?" a voice asked.

"Captain Williams, please."

"He's not in."

"Is he on his cell? This is urgent."

"May I ask who's calling?"

"Sheriff Ted Crawford."

"Hold please."

He shouldn't have let Bobbie Ann go. It made no sense at all, but he trusted Clarke, even though he'd just met him. Maybe it was their shared distrust of Colonel Anderson, and the subsequent destruction and mayhem that seemed to follow him around. Still, it made no sense, and Clarke was a bad guy for sure.

It did seem like top secret bullshit. If what Clarke said was true, this was beyond personal. The hold seemed to go on forever. A deputy knocked and he waved him in. "What's up Frank?"

"Just got a call from the EMTs. They're headed up to Ray's place."

"What for?"

"Gunshot wound. He told them some guy named Clarke shot him."

"What?"

"Said it was an accident but wanted you to know."

"Thanks. Let me know when they get him back to town."

"Will do."

Still on hold he stared at the receiver. Doubt clouded his quickly formed opinion of Clarke. Should he even go through with this call? "Williams here."

"Gary, it's Ted."

"What's going on? They said it was urgent. I'm a bit busy, so it better be."

"I got a tip. There's a threat on the event tonight, at least I think so."

"You think so? Listen, I'm up to my ass in dignitaries and

trying to reassure them. We've received dozens of threats. How solid is your information?"

"Iffy, but enough to have me concerned. Listen, are you guys handling security?"

"No, Reverend Benjamin hired his own, a private firm."

"Well, just tip them off to be extra alert."

"What kind of threat? Bomb? Assassination?"

"I don't know. Do you know if they're using canines?"

"Don't know. Why do you ask?"

"I'm not even sure. There's just been some crazy stuff going on up here, and I think some of the old white supremacist crews may be running around."

"The Aryans? Hell, there are hardly any left in the state, and none with real pull."

"I'm not so sure about that. Anyway, just wanted to pass along the information. Says some Colonel Anderson might be involved."

"Colonel Mike Anderson? No way. I know the man, and he's a bit odd, but not an Aryan."

"You're sure?"

"Yeah. Besides, he's on leave out of state last I heard. Fishing somewhere."

"Really?"

"Yeah. Listen, I have to run, but thanks for passing on the tip. I'll pass along your vague suspicions that something might happen."

The line went dead. He felt like an idiot. Ray was shot, supposedly by Clarke. He passed along a threat, one among many, that had no substance. Just a "be careful." Like they weren't doing that already. And the nonsense asking about the canines? What did he mean by that?

He shook his head and went out to the office.

"Frank, I'm going down to the cafe. Call me the minute Ray arrives."

He needed some time out of the office to clear his head. The cafe was within walking distance. As he rounded the corner of the building, he saw movement at the edge of his vision. Suddenly cautious, he turned. On the next street over he saw what could only be described as a pack of dogs, many of whom he vaguely recognized, running south. There was no time to count them.

A moment later they were gone. By the time he reached the cafe a block and a half away, he'd convinced himself that he'd imagined the whole thing.

"KEEPING THE TRUCK IS A BAD IDEA."

"I know." Glancing at her, I could tell she didn't like me, but if we found out anything about what was going on, having a reporter handy who had sources to call to get the word out could be useful. She wasn't motivated by her like or dislike of me anyway, her only motive was getting the story. Her eyes were hungry.

I always wondered about that. Reporters and writers of all kinds dedicated their entire lives to telling the story. Hell, my whole life had been spent living the story. Time after time, killing to near death, victory to defeat, sunshine in the jungle to rain on the beaches, my life had been one long plot with sad ending after sad ending. The only thing I'd ever wanted was a love story, and I'd thought I gotten that with Marsha. At least I'd had a shot at the happily ever after. Looking ahead, a happy ending seemed less and less probable.

"Did you do it?" she asked as we got closer to the city. The mountains gave way to hills, and the rendezvous point was coming up soon.

"Did I do what?"

"Did you kill that cop?"

"I did. It was self-defense, but I did."

"Did something feel weird about the whole thing?"

"What do you mean?" The road curved frequently as it descended so I couldn't look at her properly, but I risked a glance, and she seemed to be studying me.

"I mean a kid on a skateboard falls off a freeway overpass in the middle of nowhere, and his dad is the first cop on the scene."

"Unlucky, I guess."

"Yeah." She went quiet, and I glanced in the mirror at the bed of the pickup. Sparky seemed to be napping, rocked back and forth by the road.

I concentrated on the road ahead as we made a sweeping left. At a stoplight I turned on my signal and made a left. "Mind if I ask where we're going?"

"To meet a friend."

"Who's this Colonel Anderson?"

"A guy I was investigating as part of my job in the Army. I got caught. No direct evidence led to him, and I was captured and nearly killed. I escaped, got chaptered out on disability, and his connections got buried. He sent me a warning at my wedding, but I hadn't seen him or even thought of him until it became clear my pursuers were a little more than bounty hunters and clearly had some more sophisticated help."

"And shooting Ray?"

"An accident, nothing more."

"Those seem to happen a lot around you."

"I'm a warrior, trained by the best. When I'm threatened, I act. I don't think until it's over. Besides that..." I stopped.

"Besides that?"

"Nothing. I just want this to be over, and to be back with my wife. I want normal again."

"I'm not sure this is the way to make that happen."

"Me either."

I turned into the shopping center parking lot and parked in one of the outside spaces. Sparky sat up, looking around, confused. He shook his head, hopped down, and stretched mightily before walking over to pee on one of the bushes.

"What time is it?" she asked.

"Three."

"The event starts at seven."

"Thanks for pointing that out."

"Four hours. I'm just saying."

"We're close. We'll figure it out."

Just then a black SUV pulled up. It stopped next to the truck and Wilson got out. "Heard someone around here needs some help?"

I moved to him, grasping his hand to shake it, and allowing him to pull me into a hug. The click of a camera shutter startled me, and his weapon came out.

"Who's this?" The muzzle of his weapon didn't waver from the center of her chest. "Bobbie Ann. She's a reporter, and she's going to help us."

"No pictures, not of me, understood?"

"Sure," she said, calmer than I expected.

Wilson lowered the weapon, and Sparky ran over, wagging his tail and waiting to be introduced.

"This must be your goddamn dog."

"Sure is. This is Sparky. He and his friends have saved my life more than once in the last two days."

"Tell me about it on the way. That's funny. A dog helped Marsha too. Got himself killed in the process. I didn't even know you guys had a dog."

"We don't."

Sparky looked at me and whined. "Where did her rescuer come from?"

"I don't know. He was with her by the time I got to her. Wasn't wearing a collar but looked like he had one at some point."

I glanced over at Sparky. He looked like a normal dog at the moment.

He's not. There's something underneath that's different.

Wilson opened the back door and moved some things

around. "Sorry ma'am, I didn't know we had company." He glared at her.

"I'll be fine," she said, and hopped in next to duffel bags with all the hardware hidden inside. Sparky jumped up and scrambled over her lap, making a space on top of the bags.

I filled Wilson in on the little I knew as we took the back roads around the downtown area, avoiding the heavy police presence. Up ahead, the walls of the stadium rose into the afternoon sky.

———

DALE CHECKED HIS WATCH. Fucking three-fifteen.

Pedaling his bike faster, he stayed on the far side of the river.

If I see something, I'll call. If not, fuck that guy. I'm leaving. The only reason he'd agreed to help was for Ricky.

He believed Clarke's story about how his dog had died. Sure, it could have been made up, but it rang true. There was something about the guy that he just trusted, a warrior to warrior instinct he couldn't deny. The green belt wandered through the trees and toward a bridge. Just on this side, six vehicles were backed into parking spaces, all with the word Security in big letters on the side. He ducked his head, hiding his face as he rode closer. Beside the trucks were two huge U-Haul trucks.

What the hell?

He rode closer, slowing, and then it happened. "Dale Fischer?"

"Hiya, Bruce," he said.

"What are you doing? I thought for sure you would be in on this gig."

"I've been out of town and I guess I didn't get the message." Dale replied.

"Bummer."

"What are you doing?"

"Security for the big rally tonight. Just setting up now. We got some last-minute help, too."

"Really?"

"Yeah, a military guy with a few dozen men, hired by Iron-Clad today." To his right, he saw movement. He turned.

"Hello there, Fischer." Colonel Anderson said.

Dale turned. "Hi there, Colonel."

"So you've met."

"Briefly," Dale said. "I don't want to hold you guys up. You look pretty busy. I'll just be on my way."

"Nonsense, Fischer. Why don't you join me? I have a couple of questions a man with your expertise may be able to answer." The Colonel took him by the arm.

Glancing at Bruce, Dale saw he really had no options. "Go ahead, Colonel."

"Right this way." He followed the Colonel over toward what looked like a SWAT van, a ball of ice sitting where his heart had been moments before. He fingered the phone in his pocket, his instincts screaming for him to run, his feet unable to comply.

TWO DOGS RAN out into the road, and the driver brought the stake bed truck to a screeching halt. They sat in the road for a moment, and he stared at them, but they seemed unwilling to move, so he edged forward, approaching. One of the dogs jumped when he honked, the other didn't flinch or move at all. He leaned out the window and whistled between his teeth.

"Move!"

Neither flinched.

"Goddamn it," he swore. "I got no time for this shit!" Intending to physically move them, he flung the driver's door open.

The dogs stared at him for a minute longer, and then, as if

responding to a signal from someone, moved off the road and out of the way.

"Fuckers!" He shook his fist at them as he slid back in and gunned the motor before moving on, already running late to pick up some fertilizer in Boise.

CHAPTER SEVENTEEN

Marsha stopped at the intersection. "Which way, boy?"

The dog hesitated for a moment. A horn beeped behind her. He cocked his head, seemingly listening to something, then barked at her window. Left, toward Military Reserve Park.

She took the turn, covering the distance to the park in little time at all, and pulling into the parking lot. There were the usual bike rack-clad cars and SUVs and a small army of dogs sat where the archery range had been, near where two trails joined each other.

Pulling into one of many empty spaces, she shoved her car into park. Three-thirty. The kids were fresh out of school, most of their parents still at work. The parking area was sparsely populated with vehicles. Opening the door, she stepped out into the afternoon heat. The dog shot out past her and headed for the gathering of dogs. She followed.

There were at least three dozen animals, and only two or three owners. A few dogs ran around, but the majority sat in ranks, as if waiting for some signal, or word from some unseen leader. "Her" dog went and joined the rest.

"What the hell is this?" A man approached her, puzzlement twisting his otherwise pleasant face. He wore hiking boots and carried a walking stick.

"I have no idea." She moved into the area and surveyed the dogs with a keen eye. Many wore collars. Some had rumpled patches of fur where collars had recently rested.

They sat relatively still in similar poses as if all under the same "sit" and "stay" commands.

Another half dozen dogs ran into the park and joined the rest, starting another row. The man shook his head and called out to one of the dogs.

"C'mon Trapper."

An Aussie mix, it looked at him almost apologetically, but stayed sitting with the others.

The few other owners present looked puzzled as well. A chorus of called dog names got no response.

"What the hell?" the man said again.

The four humans stood, dumbfounded, watching as moments passed and more dogs came to join the formation, falling in with military precision.

Marsha still had no idea where Todd might be, and whether this was a good sign or not.

As they stood watching, two dogs detached themselves and moved out to block the road.

A stake bed truck swerved around a corner just within sight, and motored toward them. The driver shook his fist out the cab window and swerved into the parking lot, screeching to a stop. Cursing loudly he pounded the interior roof of the truck with both fists.

Out of the back at least two dozen mutts of varying sizes and uncertain parentage exited the truck and joined the growing assembly. The two dogs that had blocked the road rejoined them.

"What the fuck!" Marsha heard him shout. He slid from the driver's seat and stormed toward her.

"Those your dogs?"

"Not exactly." She answered. Why he thought she might have a few dozen dogs that were all hers was a puzzle of its own.

"What the hell's going on here?"

"We have no idea."

"Well, I'm calling somebody." He looked around wildly.

"Who?"

"Two dogs stopped my goddamn truck on the highway, and all the way through town dogs blocked the roads, leading me here. Then a whole mess of dogs just poured out the back. I didn't even know they were there. I'm calling some-goddamn-body!"

"Go ahead, pal. I'm not sure anyone will do you any good. Those dogs aren't hurtin' a thing," said the man who had approached her earlier.

"So what are you gonna do?"

"Watch. They're all waitin' for something, and I figure I'll wait too and see what it is."

The new arrival threw his sweat-stained, beer logoed hat to the ground, and stomped on it three or four times. He then picked it up, put it back on his head, and climbed into his truck, roaring away in a cloud of black smoke. They watched him go.

"I wonder what's next?" Marsha said.

They didn't have to wonder for long, as the wail of sirens approached the park. A few of the dogs started to howl, and then they began to move as one.

———

"WHY ARE WE STOPPING?" Reverend Benjamin asked his driver.

"There's a dog in the road."

"Well, move him."

"Benjamin?" his wife touched his arm.

"It's nothing Annabelle."

"You sound nervous."

"I am. For some reason, I have a bad feeling about this."

"Sir?" The driver called back.

"Yes?"

"There are several dogs in the way now. We're going to reroute, so we won't be late."

"Do what you need to. Keep me informed."

The phone by his elbow chirped, and he answered it. "Reverend, I have the Governor for you."

"Put him on."

"Ben?"

"Yes, Sir?"

"We're going to be late. This is going to sound funny, but there's a pack of dogs in the parking garage. I can't get to my car."

"What? There are dogs blocking some of the roads too."

"I know. We've called animal control, but they're swamped. Runaways and stray dogs are all over the place."

"Where are they all coming from?"

"We don't know. A chopper will pick me up in a few minutes, but it took a bit to get one ready. We'll just have less prep time than we planned."

"Okay, see you when you get there." As he hung up the motorcade slowed to a stop again, and he saw another line of dogs through the window as they made what he was sure was an unplanned right turn.

"What's going on, Colonel?"

"I'd like to ask you the same. What are you doing here, Dale?"

"Riding my bike, what does it look like?"

"Hmm. I heard about your men. I'm sorry. I never thought it would come to that. Clarke has lost his mind."

"My men, and my dog."

"Your dog?"

"Yeah, he's gone too. Killed by some soldiers in another failed raid. Seems you were busy, unless you want to pretend you don't know about any of that. Who were you really after?"

"Just Clarke."

"Seems like a lot of trouble for a guy who jumped bail."

"He's a dangerous man, you saw that for yourself."

"I saw a pack of dogs devastate my men, not Clarke."

"He did seem to have some help. How was it that your dog was involved?"

"I don't know, and it doesn't matter. What are you up to Colonel?"

"I'm on leave. Helping these boys with some security."

"I heard you were off fishing."

"Maybe I'm taking a break from the river. Doing a favor for some friends."

"Some break. Do you have those questions? If not, I'll just be on my way."

"I think I need you to stay."

"No thanks."

"We'll need your help for a couple of hours."

"I'm really busy. Have a dinner engagement after my ride."

"I'm afraid it will have to wait." Colonel Anderson folded his arms over his chest.

"Are you threatening me?"

"No, merely assuring myself that you aren't a threat to the festivities tonight."

"Me, a threat?"

"I think you have connections with Aryan extremists and should be detained until we can more fully investigate your background."

"I think you have me confused with you, Colonel."

"Please, call me Mike. And I think you'll find that the men

with me will be on my side. Cooperate, and there will be no need for your wait to be...unpleasant."

"I really think—"

The door to the truck opened, and Dale felt himself lifted from his chair. "Make sure you get his phone. Don't rough him up unless he makes that necessary. Understood?"

Two men nodded and guided him out. "Right this way, Sir."

As they passed one of the moving trucks, he looked in the open back door. Inside, sitting on benches up against the wall were about a dozen men, clad in body armor and armed with assault rifles.

———

EVER SINCE 9/11 security forces were better briefed and prepared for urban-type warfare. Hell, the Orchard Training Center had a permanent Urban Training Center, and a firing range known as the Boston Townhouse. Local private security teams trained there often. Hiring them was costly, but they were more efficient and certainly better prepared than local police, and it left the police force free to secure the streets and more public areas around a venue.

Their availability was a secondary effect of the downsizing of the military and the retirement of relatively young veterans of Gulf Wars One and Two who really had no other profession than that of warrior. They made perfect security and private police-men, programmed to follow orders without question and with the necessary skills to handle nearly any situation.

The men of IronClad Security were no exception. They took their jobs seriously, and protected dignitaries frequently, even working with the Secret Service. Started as a local firm, now teams were sent nationwide, and recently internationally.

As a result, they were spread thin on this job, booked at the last minute by Reverend Benjamin, and so they'd welcomed the help of Colonel Anderson and his men.

A truck pulled up, and several men exited and filed into the small entrance.

"Do a final sweep of the stadium floor and the stage areas," the man in charge ordered.

The men fanned out and he watched as they used electronic scanners that reminded him of the tricorders of the old Star Trek shows to search. He wished they had bomb-sniffing dogs, but that was an aspect of the business his company was not yet into.

The men moved in a smooth formation, spread over the entire lower stadium area, moving with military precision toward the stage, their search areas slightly overlapping. As they reached the edge, four men ducked under the scaffolding to check underneath.

His phone chirped, and he turned away. The men were as competent as the Colonel had promised, and he had other matters to attend to.

———

THE MEN DUCKED under the stage and waited for the signal from the men still "scanning" the area for explosives.

A knock came from above.

They didn't say a word but exchanged hand signals. The man with the largest charge hidden in his cargo pocket crawled toward the center. Above, they could all hear boot steps as the men above checked speakers, wires, and chairs. They put on a good show. Three stomps in a row gave away the location of the podium. The soldier flipped onto his back, and deftly planted a specially shaped charge.

The other three men moved around the perimeter, attaching explosives to selected supports. The entire platform would collapse. The placed charge at the podium would directly take out the desired target, but it wouldn't look like an assassination.

They assembled in front of the stage, and the leader spoke into a radio. "Stage one complete."

"Stage two go." They heard.

As they filed out of the service door, a second truck pulled up outside. Men poured into the building, swarming the upper decks of the stadium, searching for threats.

The whole operation was designed to look precise yet a little confusing to the untrained eye. Four men that went in did not come out. Two sniper teams: each with a spotter and a gunner, one on either side of the stadium, placed themselves. Their 50 mm rifles remained unassembled in cases and they waited patiently, using their spotting scopes to pick possible shots, evaluate angles, and plan escape routes when they were discovered.

The men of IronClad were good. Some were even friends, once serving in the same units in wars misunderstood by both sides. The men had simply chosen different paths in the private security industry: Colonel Anderson paid more than other companies, and the mission did not change from operation to operation.

Every man in their group bore at least one symbol of the superiority of their race and accepted it as an unquestionable fact. They came from all over the country, many of them leading chapters of the Cause in their own hometowns, their own states.

They'd all come to Boise for the chance of a lifetime.

———

GARY HAD WORKED animal control in Boise for years. Rounder than he'd been ten years ago, he still felt he was in pretty good shape. He couldn't run as fast anymore, but he'd developed a rapport with dogs over the years. Most, except for those who were rabid or abused, he could lure into his truck with relative ease.

The reason was simple. Almost without exception, he loved the four-legged guys far better than most of the two-legged animals running around the city. Some of those chose to abuse his four-legged friends, and he loathed them.

This afternoon something was wrong with every dog in the city. Dogs that never ran away, or at least stuck to their neighborhoods were roaming all over the downtown area. Most of the dogs, even the ones he knew from their frequent forays from their homes, wouldn't respond to his usual tactics. As the day wore on, every off-duty animal control officer was activated, an unprecedented amount of overtime authorized. They couldn't keep up.

Every truck was full. Every kennel at the shelter overflowed. Almost as soon as the owner picked up a dog, it would escape and run off again, if two or three didn't get out as soon as the kennel door opened. It felt like they were all infected with some kind of fever.

Vets checked them over, and physically they were normal. Something was in their heads. It wasn't a full moon, no sunspots, no astrological anomaly seemed to be in play, yet they all seemed possessed by a singular magnetic draw. The downtown area of the greenbelt drew them, snarling traffic and inhibiting pedestrian travel. They weren't bothering anyone specifically, there were just so many of them. Pulling his truck into the parking lot of the shelter, he intended to take a short break. Today he felt his work to be ineffective, his efforts fruitless.

He stared out the window at the full lot, concerned owners striding back and forth, and shook his head.

The canine world was off, and as a result, his was too. An ominous instinct tickled at the back of his neck like a feather, telling him something was going to happen, and his mind could not ignore it.

———

"JEFFERS HERE."

"Detective Kelly," the officer said by way of introduction.

"Sorry to bother you, Sir, but we have a kid downtown here who insists on talking to you about a case you were involved in not long ago."

"So, tell him to set up an appointment."

"It's the Clarke case, Sir."

"What about it?"

"It's one of the skater kids that testified. He says he didn't exactly tell the whole truth on the stand."

"Really?"

"Yes, Sir. I think you should let the defense know too."

"I'm rather busy, and it's nearly the end of my day."

"He got caught stealing today. Says he wants to make a deal."

Jeffers looked over the files on his desk and sighed. The Clarke case was behind him. The guy ran. In his book that equaled guilt. The time for negotiations had passed. Still, something had never felt quite right there. Clarke didn't seem like the kind of guy who would run rather than stand up to consequences if he was guilty. Rockford seemed adamant on that point too.

"I'll be there in half an hour. I'll call Rockford, but no promises on that score."

Why today? He'd planned to go to the rally tonight, and it was only a couple of hours away. Hell, everyone he knew was going, and he wasn't going to miss it for some snot-nosed kid with a wild story.

He dialed Rockford. "Hey, where are you right now?"

"My office. What's up?"

"Want to meet me at the holding station in five? Detective Kelly has one of our skater kids who claims his testimony wasn't exactly truthful in the Clarke case."

"Interesting. I suppose I could clear my desk. I wanted to leave early tonight anyway and get to the rally."

"Yeah, me too. Meet me downtown and when we're done with the kid, we'll go together."

"Okay, see you in a few."

Jeffers straightened his shoulders and walked out of his office into the afternoon sun. It was a short walk from his office to police headquarters and City Hall, and then they could take a cab or retrieve his car to head to the rally. As he turned down the sidewalk, he saw there were dogs everywhere, milling between the pedestrians, sometimes unintentionally blocking the sidewalk as they marked a light pole or hydrant with territory-claiming urine.

"What the hell?" He muttered, weaving his way through them.

––––––––

Clarke set up down the block for their initial surveillance, concerned. Dale hadn't contacted him at all.

They'd seen the two trucks come and go. He counted the men going in, and then again when they came out. Four men stayed behind.

Two sniper teams.

A cop drove by twice, the second time stopping long enough to take note of their plate number. Although this vehicle would legally check out, they couldn't risk being detained, or worse having the vehicle searched. They needed somehow to blend with the rest of the crowd headed to the stadium without tipping security. It was almost five o'clock, and the event was set to start at seven. Two hours. About an hour until the doors would open and the crowds of civilians would pour inside.

They'd already started to arrive and form several lines at the metal detectors where they would be screened before entry.

The reporter dozed in the back seat, hand tangled in Sparky's fur.

"Move to the west side. We'll wait there until the crowd arrives, and then blend in."

"How?"

"Disguised as security."

"And him?" Wilson pointed to Sparky, who'd been resting and strangely quiet.

"He'll be our security dog. Still got that K-9 vest you had for Missy?"

"I think so. It should be in the same bag as the security labels for the vests, but it might be big for him. What about her?"

"She's a reporter. She should have a press card or something right? All we can do is give it a try, right boy?"

Sparky beat his tail twice on the seat but remained otherwise still.

"Right. But you'll never get in posed as security." She moved slowly, stretching.

"Why's that?"

"The company running this one is pretty strict. IronClad has special badges for their men. If you don't have one, you won't get far. They had a gig where some of the bad guys tried that somewhere else in the country. It didn't work."

"How do you know that?"

"I had a thing with the owner, Adam Larson."

"Had?'

"Yep, had. He thought I was just using him to get information on his events and clients to scoop any news."

"Were you?"

"No comment. We're still friends."

"So can you get us in?"

"Maybe Wilson here, and the dog, but not you. He's not stupid. Pretty tuned in to current events. Your face being all over the news and all, he'd recognize you unless you have a pretty good disguise handy along with a fake ID that will fool his computer geniuses."

I looked at Wilson, and he shook his head.

"So I'm supposed to trust you?" I said.

"Don't see many other options. You can join the crowd, probably get in that way, but you can't be armed, and if you move around too suspiciously you might find yourself under close scrutiny, something I'm sure you don't want."

I leaned back in the seat, thinking.

"You can use this sweatshirt of mine," she said. "It might be a little small."

"I have a crude disguise," Wilson offered. "It will have to do."

I looked at the clock on the dash. Five after five. Sparky sat up and barked.

"Call your friend, Bobbie, and see if you guys can get inside. I'll move in with the crowd and hope to hook up with you once we are inside."

"And Sparky?"

"He doesn't use K-9s yet, but I can ask."

"Ask sweetly."

I didn't like the plan, didn't like it at all, but we were out of time and options.

———

Marsha watched as the dogs exited the park, row after row, following slowly in an orderly fashion. As they left, the ranks filled with more dogs. She lost count at one- hundred and fifty.

Her mind wandered, wondering where Todd might be, how she might find him, what might be next for them both.

As she thought it, a Collie mix trotted up to her, and barked. In its mouth, it held a leash.

"Hi there." She squatted to be down on the dog's level, rubbing its head, and it dropped the leash in front of her, eyes darting to it and then back to her face. "What do you want, girl?" she asked, assuming its sex without checking.

The dog repeated the gesture, and she got it. "You want to go for a walk?" The dog barked happily, its tail wagging, and it circled around her, jumping up and striking her chest, nearly knocking her off balance.

"Okay, okay," she said, and clipped the leash to the dog's

collar as if she'd done it a thousand times. The dog led her off at a near-trot, as if in a hurry to get somewhere.

It followed the lines of other dogs, as they too scampered two by two, sometimes nipping playfully at each other, all headed the same direction.

Smiling and giggling as she was pulled along, she found she really was enjoying herself despite the odd circumstances.

CHAPTER EIGHTEEN

"Stage one and two set."

"Excellent. Begin stage three."

"Yes, Sir."

Anderson stepped out of the truck and looked around. Something was going on. Two lines of dogs marched down the street. They moved quickly, but moved in ranks, keeping even with each other, almost as if they were marching. As he watched, the lead group of dogs broke off and began to circle the parking area where he and his men were staged.

The men were already stepping out, looking around as he jogged across the parking area to the vehicles.

"What do we do, Sir?" One asked.

The dogs continued to surround their position, leaving an even distance of about three feet between each. Turning in a full circle, he saw that once a perimeter was established, the remainder of the dogs kept marching toward the bridge over the river, down the road that led to the stadium.

Movement drew his attention to the river, and he looked across to the path on the other side. Dogs marched from that direction too, moving in two rows, all headed toward the stadium.

"Get Fischer out here," he said. One of the men walked to the other armored truck and opened the door. Dale stepped out, arms still cuffed behind his back, and looked around with astonishment.

"What's happening?" he asked.

"I was hoping you'd know. All along Clarke has been protected by dogs. You seen anything like this before?"

He stared. "Not really. When we approached the compound, it was a pack of dogs, mutts like these that defended him."

"How?"

"They attacked my men. You ever notice that even the toughest cage fighters never fight a fucking dog, colonel? You know why?"

"Humor me with your wisdom."

"They're fast. If you have a gun, you can shoot them. But you have one shot. If the dog is trained well or in a rage, or even just protecting itself or its owner out of instinct, you're in trouble once they get within a certain range. You can't beat them bare handed."

"Right. So how do you neutralize them?"

Dale shrugged. "Other dogs. Whistles. Gas. Stuff you have to be prepared with."

"What about these dogs?"

"They don't appear to be trained. See all the collars? They belong to people. They're responding to something, though."

"What? Clarke is dead."

Dale hesitated. "Whatever it was at that compound, it wasn't Clarke."

"How do you know that?"

"I just do."

He grabbed Dale by the collar. "Tell me how the hell you know?"

"My dog saved me, but then he joined up with those dogs when your men attacked. It's the only thing that makes sense. Clarke had nothing to do with that."

"What did?"

"How the fuck would I know? Who or what would my dog die for, but me? I don't know, Colonel, and if I did, I don't know that I'd tell you. You answer that yourself. What are you really doing here? Why are these dogs surrounding you and your men? What are you doing that they would die to stop? You tell me, who would command them, control them to stop it?"

Colonel Anderson didn't answer, but he shouted orders into his radio. Men disembarked from the trucks and formed a tight armed perimeter. The ranks of dogs sat just outside, forming their own circle looking in.

On the street, two trucks were trapped by the dogs and traffic, unable to pull back in. The Colonel barked another set of orders into his radio, and they pulled off, disappearing from view.

Dale smiled to himself. Despite the fact that he was cuffed in the middle of a group of domestic terrorists, he felt safe.

———

"Why'd you lie, son?" Jeffers asked

"Tyler asked us to. His dad too. And they offered us money," Tommy answered.

"Money?"

"Yeah."

"So why tell us now? Just because you're in trouble?"

"I took the board because I ain't got paid yet, and I'm tired of waitin'."

"So Tyler didn't really die?"

"Nope."

"Where'd the body come from then?"

"Some Army dudes dropped it off to us."

"Army dudes?"

"I think they were. They wore camouflage, and they called Tyler's dad Sergeant."

"Sergeant? He wasn't a sergeant?"

"Tyler said they were with The Cause when I asked."

"The Cause?" A chill ran down his spine.

"Yeah. Something and his dad were really into. He tried to talk to me about it once, but it was too confusing."

"Confusing?"

"Yeah, and when I told him my great-grandmother was a Jew, he told me my blood was probably tainted anyway. What did he mean by that?"

"I'm not sure." Jeffers cleared his throat. "Did he say why you were doing what you were?"

"Nope. Just that the guy deserved it. I never dreamed the dude would shoot his dad like that."

"So where's Tyler now?"

"Don't know. He was supposed to call. Never did. Just like we never got paid."

"The other kids didn't get paid either?"

"Nope, but they didn't need it as bad as I do."

"You know where they live?"

"Yeah, sure."

"Can you give their addresses to the officer here?"

Tommy wrote them down on a yellow legal pad. Jeffers had him clarify some of the numbers and letters that he could not read.

"So can I go now?"

"Why don't you hang here for a while? Wait until we bring in your friends? That way we can talk to you all at the same time."

"Okay, I guess, but am I still in trouble over the board?"

"We'll talk about that one later, okay?"

"Sure." Tommy looked down at his hands.

Jeffers and Rockford left the room together. "What do you make of that?"

"I don't know, but I have someone I can call and ask some questions."

"Do it." Jeffers glanced at his watch. "Hell, maybe we'll still make it tonight."

"Maybe, but I've never been much for being a part of history anyway."

"Me either." They both laughed.

Jeffers went in search of coffee, and Rockford searched his phone, settling on a number and dialing.

———

IT WAS HARD TO MOVE. Dogs surrounded the car. Wilson lowered the window so Sparky could stick his head out. He barked what sounded like commands, and the dogs parted just enough so we could pass.

Finally, we parked, and as I opened the door Sparky sprinted away into the crowd of dogs. Other early arrivals tried to pull in to park. Down the road, a convoy of official- looking vehicles swung around the corner slowly, seemingly escorted by a pack of dogs.

I looked around. There were hundreds of mutts, roaming everywhere. A block away, I spotted someone moving toward us through the crowd with a dog on a leash.

Bobbie Ann slid from the back seat, ending a call on her cell. "C'mon Wilson, we're in, sort of. I'll explain on the way. You're allowed one sidearm."

"One?" He looked with longing at the bags in the back.

"Those will have to wait." She turned to me. "Remember how recognizable you are. Adam can't control the cops, or his guys if they perceive you as a threat. Keep your head down."

I nodded and mumbled an affirmative, distracted.

As Bobbie and Wilson moved off, I searched the sea of fur for Sparky's familiar coat, missing him when he wasn't at my side. I opened the back, grabbing the hooded sweatshirt, and slipped it over my head despite the warm evening. Scanning the crowd, I spotted the dog walker closer than before. The form looked incredibly familiar.

It can't be.

No one else had that walk. That body.

That look.

It had to be. I moved forward, and then broke into a run at the same time she did. We met halfway, and I grabbed her, smelled her, touched her.

I looked down and saw a Collie mix, leash trailing behind her, bouncing around our feet as if asking, "Did I do good? Did I do good?"

I looked into Marsha's eyes, and we kissed with the eager passion of time lost, while around us dogs barked, whimpered, growled, and moved together in a protective circle.

———

Colonel Andreson's personal phone chirped, although he could hardly hear it over the crowd and the chaos of the dogs. He looked around. Nearly everyone that had that number was there, with him.

He answered. "What?"

"It's Rockford. Where's Clarke?"

"Rockford? What?"

"Your man Clarke? Where is he?"

"We've been over this. I don't know."

"I think you do. I know you want to protect him, but new information has come to light."

"New information?"

"One of the kids. Downtown now, telling us his testimony was fake. I need to talk to Clarke."

"I'm afraid I'm a bit busy right now, Mr. Rockford. And I can't help you. We'll talk later."

As he spoke, a chorus of howling erupted from the dogs'

throats as sirens sounded. A trio of fire engines headed toward the stadium, and he couldn't imagine why.

"Where are you?"

He hung up and turned to look back. People wandered down the street, moving in and through the parade of dogs, everyone headed to the stadium. Things were going sideways fast.

A dog blocked his path back to the SWAT van, teeth bared, growling. Anderson pulled his sidearm, and then stepped back, looking around.

The soldier from Wyoming approached.

Speaking softly to his dog, he tried to coax it away, but it ignored him, and wouldn't move.

"Get that dog out of my way, son, or I'll have to kill it."

"Trying, Sir." The man moved to her side, stroking her fur. The dog calmed, her hackles falling, and she sat next to his side.

She growled softly at the Colonel as he walked by.

"Well?" Jeffers asked.

"Something's wrong."

"Really? You think so? Thanks for stating the obvious."

"No. My source is here in town. I heard sirens in the background."

"So?"

"It doesn't feel right. He still claims to not know where Clarke is, and—"

"And?" Jeffers sipped his coffee and offered Rockford a cup.

"I don't know. What's with all the dogs in town?" Rockford drank. The coffee was strong and good.

"I don't know that either."

"What should we do now?"

"Wait for the kids?"

"And then?"

"I have no idea. The whole situation is fucked. Without

Clarke, without the trooper and his son, we got the word of a pissed off, in trouble skater kid to go on. But I believe him."

"Me too."

"I've got one more call to make. I'll be right back."

"Take your time," Jeffers said. "I don't think we're going anywhere."

———

THE COLLIE only tolerated our greeting for so long. It jumped around our feet, barking. When I looked down, she was holding the end of the leash in her mouth and wagging her tail.

"What?" I asked.

"She wants to lead us," Marsha said. "That's how I found you." I looked around again for Sparky, but he was still nowhere to be found.

"Okay girl," I said, crouching next to her. "Lead the way."

Her eyes sparkled as I grabbed the leash and she took off, pulling me along. Marsha took my hand, staying close. Up ahead, I saw that the convoy with the limo in the middle had finally made it into the parking lot, and overhead I heard a chopper. The dignitaries had arrived.

My feet seemed to move on their own as the dog dragged us forward. The stadium loomed, and I could hear sirens on the other side. I wondered what was happening over there, but I couldn't stop or take my eyes off our path for long as dogs darted around in front of and around us.

Ten feet away from a set of service doors, our guide stopped, and I almost stepped on her before realizing it, and then all of the air rushed from my lungs.

The dogs surrounded the stadium, spaced about five feet apart, two deep. There wasn't a person inside the circle I could see. To my right a man tried to dart forward, and a dog growled loudly. He persisted and the dog snapped at his outstretched leg. The man retreated. To the left I saw a commotion as four young people tried to press forward. The dogs gathered and formed a fur barrier, barring the way with teeth bared and hackles raised.

The Collie looked up at me, and I released her leash. She moved around, filling in a hole with the others. Still, there was no sign of Sparky. Holding Marsha's hand, I crept slowly forward. The dogs parted in front of us and allowed us to walk ahead. I heard a scuffle behind and turned to see someone try to follow. The dogs quickly closed the gap, still defending the perimeter. An instinct propelled me toward the service doors, and when we reached them, I found them unlocked.

"Todd, what are you doing?" Marsha whispered.

"I'm not sure, but it's what I need to do. It's why they brought me here." I gestured at the dogs around the building. "You don't have to come along."

"They saved me too," she said. "There has to be a reason."

I scanned the upper levels of the stadium for sniper perches. There had to be something else. No way would Anderson bet everything on two sniper teams. I looked to the stadium floor and the stage. A reddish dog that looked like Sparky sat in the center next to the podium.

"Hold it right there!"

Turning, I saw a security guard, a well-trained one by his manner, pointing a gun at us. "Let me see some hands."

I stood slowly, and he walked forward, pistol ready, fingering two sets of zip tie cuffs from a pocket on the leg of his uniform pants.

————

HIS PHONE CHIRPED AGAIN. "ANDERSON."

"It's Adam. I need a support team."

"We're kind of occupied. What's going on?"

"This is why we hired you and let you in on this one. I thought you were staged nearby."

"We are. We are just hemmed in by the crowd and some...animals."

"Us too. We have dogs surrounding the entire building, two deep, not letting anyone in. We have fire trucks here, ready to sweep them away with hoses if need be, but we need some help with crowd control."

"We'll be there when we can. Meanwhile, get those water cannons on those dogs." He surveyed the circle within his vision, and saw his men facing off with dogs who at the moment sat quietly watching.

"Call as soon as you arrive."

"Sure," he said, hanging up. There was no pretty way out of this. Killing some dogs and maybe some people, maybe even some of his own men seemed inevitable.

He went over the layout in his mind. There were only two bridges within a reasonable distance. One took both vehicle and foot traffic, one was only for pedestrians. He'd picked this location to be isolated from the stadium and the blast, far enough removed not to be suspected, at least not immediately.

Now his plans were disrupted, and he needed to get there and handle things personally.

Across the river, a helicopter circled, and landed in an empty lot right beside the water.

As he watched, a group of mutts separated from the others, and surrounded it in a tight circle.

Then the idea came. He moved away from the circle of dogs and back to the truck holding the command center. Timing was everything.

———

JED AND WILL were busy shredding it. Sweat rolled off their bodies.

Jed entered the half-pipe and hit the edge, doing a one-handed stand, extending his board over his head, keeping it next to his feet. As his body swung downward, he brought the board back down and landed, rolling on the curved surface toward the other side. Elevating over the side with a quick tail-grab 180, he rolled further down the pipe, gaining momentum. Jumping out, he twisted his body once, and then halfway around again. His feet missed the board, and it clattered into the center of the pipe as he slid down the side on his ass, gloved hands pounding the cement in frustration.

"You almost nailed it, dude."

"Almost doesn't count."

"Sure it does. C'mon, one more time, and then it's my turn."

He climbed out of the pipe, and they walked toward the skate park entrance. "You seen Tommy?"

"Nope, not today."

"Thought sure as shit he'd be here with a new board, he was so anxious to blow that hundred."

"I sent him a text, but no answer."

"Bummer dude." He set up to launch again.

A voice from behind them spoke. "Hi there, boys."

They turned together and a man stood facing them dressed in some kind of military uniform. "You guys haven't seen Tommy, have you?"

"Nope."

"Well, I've got your money for you, and his too."

The boys high fived and walked toward him. "Cool shit bro. It's about time."

The man just smiled as they got closer, and reached behind his back, pulling a pistol, with a long cylinder on the end they both knew from the movies to be a silencer.

"Oh shit!" Will dived for the ground, but before he even hit, saw a blur of fur and heard a snarl and growl. The whisper of a silenced shot was chased by the sound of it ricocheting through the half pipe.

A large dog sat on the man's chest, the man's pistol discarded in the grass. Half of the man's cheek lay open, revealing his teeth and his moving jaw. An odd sound reached them both, and they realized it was him trying to scream.

They looked at each other and backed away, turning to run. "Hold it!"

Expecting the worst, they turned. A cop stood there, staring at the scene, gun drawn.

"Jesus!" he said. "You kids okay?"

His hands shook, and they could hardly hear him over the high-pitched scream of the soldier who had approached them.

The fallen man's eyes went wide in terror and he struggled to reach his dropped weapon.

Time slowed. His fingers touched the pistol, and the dog lunged off his chest, grabbing his wrist in its powerful jaws. Blood spurted.

The cop fired, the shot echoing through the concrete structures of the skate park, and the dog yelped, its body jerking. It rolled away, landing on its side, desperately panting for air. Blood poured from a hole in its hind leg.

Jed leapt to his feet and ran to the dog's side. The cop just stood there, clearly in shock, as the wounded man jerked once, twice, and lay still, blood pooling around his head and arm.

Silence reigned for a moment, and then the cop dropped to his knees and vomited. Taking in the scene, he spoke into his radio.

"Shots fired. Officer requesting assistance, assailant down."

"Say again."

"Officer requesting assistance, shots fired."

"Copy that. Help is on the way."

The radio went silent, and the only sounds were the dog's ragged breaths, and

Jed's quiet sobbing.

CHAPTER NINETEEN

I didn't want to hurt him.

But he threatened me, her, and the mission, so he had to be neutralized. I raised my hands at his approach. He was alone, and apparently hadn't used his radio yet.

He stopped less than ten feet away. "How'd you get in? The gates don't open until six."

"The door was unlocked," Marsha said.

Good girl. Defuse the situation. Offer him a distraction, an innocent explanation.

"You'll have to come with me. This is a restricted area."

She looked around. "I didn't see any signs."

"I'm instructed to question anyone found in this area. I'm just doing my job, ma'am. I'm sure it won't take long."

Concentrating on her, the guard did not see me approach from the side, grabbing his arm and twisting it up behind him. He dropped his pistol, but recovered quickly.

I circled carefully, leading him away from Marsha.

He struck first, a near direct hit. As I ducked the first punch, a second followed, contacting my jaw and rattling my focus. I brought my hands up in defense and struck out with my left foot. The kick struck the back of his thigh, and his leg forced my foot downward. Keeping my balance, I went on the offensive. Swinging a wide, distracting punch, I pulled it short as he moved to defend, and stepped inside his reach, delivering short sharp punches to his body designed to wear him down. Under his uniform, I felt body armor that enabled him to take the punches easily. He spun away. I felt out of practice, and clearly he wasn't.

I blocked a low kick followed by another, and another. We danced, moving back and forth, each looking for an opening, each blocking blow after blow, kick after kick, slipping from the other's grasp. Fists struck air or hardened muscle. The wound in my leg ached, and involuntarily I started to limp, unable to hide the pain any longer.

He moved in tighter as I tired, but I slowed deliberately. Taking a solid kick to my leg, I staggered sideways and nearly fell. Moving in to subdue me, he dropped his guard for a second. Bringing my fist up, I struck him below his vest, just above his groin. Unprepared this time, he doubled over. I grabbed the back of his neck and brought my wounded knee up into his face. The stitched wound reopened, but his nose shattered. Striking again with my bad leg, I kicked him solidly in the groin. As he bent at the waist again, I hopped forward, stumbling but steadying myself the best I could. He straightened but his eyes were glassy, his face contorted in pain.

I brought my elbow around, struck his temple, and sent him sprawling. As he fell, I collapsed across his back, lifting his chin.

"No!" Marsha hissed. "Stop!"

My leg ached, my knuckles were bruised, my elbow bled from the conflict. Grabbing a set of zip-tie cuffs from his pocket, I secured his wrists and studied the scene.

The fight had taken place under a bleacher area, out of sight of the rest of the stadium. I dragged him from sight, listening carefully. So far, there were no sounds of responding help.

Then I heard voices arguing way off to my right, and I grabbed Marsha's hand and pulled her into hiding.

Peeking around the edge of this section of bleachers, I saw a dog far away that looked like Sparky sitting in the center of the stage, unmoving.

———

"We have to call it off," one voice said.

"We are not canceling the rally," The new governor said.

"But Governor—"

"You talk to Benjamin about this?"

"Yes, Sir."

"And what did he say?"

The security officer looked at his shoes.

"That's what I thought. Get those dogs out of here, and get those people in. History will not be stopped by a pack of stray dogs and some paranoid security people that think some nutty, solo, ex-soldier cop-killer can take the whole thing down."

"But Sir, this could be a legitimate threat. My source—"

"Fuck your source, and fuck anyone else who wants to stop this. Would any other Governor hide from this kind of threat?"

"Sir, it's the Aryan connection. Something called the cause."

"So it's because I'm black, and I'm backed nationally?"

"No sir. Regardless, we have to look at the possibility that this threat is real."

"Real or not, I won't be chased off this stage by fear. Otherwise, every time I have a public appearance of any importance, a threat will shut it down, and they win. Does that sound practical to you? Like I would be seen as a capable Governor?"

"No, Sir."

"Then you get your shit together, get these people together, meet with these private security pukes, the cops, everyone. You get those gates open, those people in here, and you get this thing started, and you get it started on time. One more word about canceling, and you're fired. Understand?"

"Yes, Sir."

"Jesus!" He swore as the man walked away. "What kind of spineless joke do they think I am?"

"Sir?"

"Never mind. Did they get Ben and Annabelle inside yet?"

"Yes."

"Take me to them."

"Yes, Sir."

———

"Tell those people to get back," the police sergeant told a second officer.

"And if they don't?"

"Then they get wet, and maybe blown around a bit."

"This sucks, Sarge. I don't want to do it."

"Either the fire department lets them have it with the hoses and chases them off or we have to come in with rubber bullets, Tasers, and God knows what else. They'll probably kill some of them. This is the most merciful method. Besides, I didn't ask. I gave you an order."

He raised the bullhorn to his lips at the same time he heard an announcement on from the other parking area on the east side.

"Fall back. We're going to clear the dogs from the area. Fall back." A few people grumbled. Raised fists in anger. Most complied.

The few that didn't would soon enough.

"Ready hoses. Three, two, one," he heard. Looking around, he saw the looks on the faces of the firemen. None of them wanted to do this.

The hoses came on. As always they seemed to want to leap form the hands of those controlling them, and wave around like in the cartoons, but the firemen stood fast as the pressure from the hydrants steadied.

A few dogs were bowled over, tossed from their feet. Yips and whines came from some as droplets pierced their fur. Loud barking started and then stopped. Almost as a unit the dogs remaining on their feet pulled back, turning tail and trotting away. A line formed behind the stadium along the river about 150 yards away. A second line formed, as more dogs joined the furry formation.

"Cut in three, two, one." At once the water stopped, but the dogs remained where they were. A few lay on the pavement, panting and clearly injured by the pressurized water. Others managed to limp toward the two lines, joining the ranks.

A large wolf Husky mix made his way over, one eye bleeding, panting, several scrapes on his side oozing blood. The crowd seemed to hold its collective breath, unable to look away. He stepped to a position at what looked like the center of the group of dogs, raised his head, and barked twice. He took a ragged breath, and barked twice more.

The barks echoed over the heads of the crowd, off the walls of the stadium, over the water.

As a unit the two columns of dogs turned, and walked west, down the trail that paralleled the river.

"Sarge," the fireman dropped the megaphone to his side. "Did you see that?"

"Yes," came the quiet response.

"What just happened?"

"I have no idea."

The paralysis in the crowd broke, and security took up their positions at the entrances and screening lines It was exactly six o'clock, the scheduled time for the gates to open. People poured inside by the hundreds and then the thousands, the VIPs directed to the floor area and the hundreds of folding chairs there, the rest filling the stadium seats, checking their tickets for rows, seats, numbers, calling to friends and family. Vendors walked the aisles, selling programs and answering questions.

———

Bobbie Ann waited in the women's restroom, not sure what else to do. Wilson was off talking to Adam, and she wanted to feel useful.

No matter what the threat, neither man would call off the rally this evening. She thought maybe she could appeal to the sensibilities of a woman.

It still might do no good, but at the least she could get close to Annabelle. Maybe get an interview. The more she looked around at how tight the security was, the more she saw of Adam and his men, the more she thought Clarke might either be wrong, or whatever anyone planned would likely be thwarted by this force. It didn't seem possible for anything to get past this.

Adam had seen her, given her a quick friend-but-we-used-to-be-more hug and disappeared, he and Wilson talking business. Wilson knew his stuff, and he seemed to possess an instant connection with some of these men. Some seemed to recognize him, acknowledging his presence with a nod.

She'd made her way inside a historic event, and she intended to use it to her advantage.

They'd searched her, of course, but she still had her cell phone camera and her notebook. A voice recording app was open, ready to go as soon as there was something worth documenting.

She looked in the mirror. Never prejudiced, she had to admit the election had surprised her. The subsequent reactions hadn't. A state once known as a hotbed for racism was now for the first time in its history truly divided by a debate not based on the qualifications of the man, but by his race.

It was wrong and backward, and against everything she believed, yet she understood. She hadn't voted for him, not because he wasn't qualified, but to avoid this.

The door opened, and Annabelle, Reverend Benjamin's wife,

walked in. She wiped her eyes, as if she'd been crying. "Excuse me," she said, and headed for a stall.

Bobbie Ann waited patiently.

Annabelle came out and moved to the sink. "Annabelle, I'm Bobbie Ann—"

"A reporter, I know. Couldn't you wait until I wasn't in the bathroom at least? Have you no respect for privacy?"

"Ma'am, this has nothing to do with privacy. Right now, I'm not here as a reporter. I just wanted to talk."

Annabelle turned and put her hands on her hips. "So talk."

"I have a friend. Well, a new friend. He says there's a threat tonight."

"We've heard all that. What kind of threat?"

"He...well he wasn't sure. But the dogs—"

"You know something about the dogs? What is going on with that? Are they part of this threat?"

"No ma'am. I think they're trying to protect you."

"Protect me?"

"You and your husband, maybe all of us."

"Why?"

"I don't know, just..."

"Just what?" Annabelle stared, hands on her hips.

"I don't know what to say. We just all share this feeling something bad is going to happen tonight."

"Based on what?"

"Instinct?" Bobbie Ann began to question herself.

"Listen, Miss..."

"Call me Bobbie."

"Whatever. Listen, we've received all kinds of threats at every event we've held supporting the Governor's campaign since the election. Nearly every day. If we listened to them, we'd never make a public appearance. I don't know you, and I don't know your friend. But I know my husband and the Governor too. We have the best security money can buy, and he's going on stage tonight. Now if you'll excuse me."

Annabelle stormed out of the bathroom. Bobbie Ann wasn't satisfied. She felt the woman's tension and her discomfort.

Something in the air, the dogs, all of it, made it clear tonight wasn't normal. She followed at a discrete distance. As Annabelle made her way to the green room, Bobbie noticed movement in the shadows. The yellow glow of a dog's eyes caught her attention, and then they were gone.

———

"WE HAVE TO FIND HIM." The pain radiated from my thigh, but I couldn't give in. Sparky had led me here, and I needed him.

"Todd, you're not thinking straight." A part of me knew she was right, but I couldn't shut it out, like an itch I had to scratch.

We took refuge in an out of the way equipment closet, and we could hear people moving around in the stands above us. It'd only be a matter of time before the guard was missed. We couldn't stay long.

Rummaging through some first aid supplies on the shelves, I found some ibuprofen and popped a couple, dry swallowing them. I needed to come up with a plan of some sort. First, I needed to figure out where we were.

Easing my way out, I saw that the area was empty. I moved slowly into the open, sensing Marsha close behind. As I did, I heard a rustling. Two dogs crept toward me cautiously. They closed the distance and moved up next to me. The first licked my hand and wagged his tail, then they both headed toward a dark hallway. I hesitated.

Turning as a unit, one moved back to me, then spun again, walking toward the hall.

"They want us to follow them," Marsha said.

"I know," I replied, still hesitant.

The second dog came back. Close, he whined softly up at me. They both walked away.

"I don't think we have any other option," Marsha said.

Knowing she was right, I held out my hand, and she took it, staying with me as I limped after the pair, hoping beyond hope that they knew more than I did.

———

"So you're telling me that thousands of people are streaming in here, and the guy I partnered with for extra security, an active military colonel, is part of the threat?"

"No, I'm telling you he is the threat."

"And you base this on the word of a friend of yours who is ex-military, special forces, did some undercover shit, and is now wanted for skipping bail on a murder charge. I should believe you why?"

"I can't make you, but if you don't at least check it out, whatever happens is on you."

"And the dogs?"

"I think they're trying to help."

"You *think*?"

"Sorry, I don't speak dog. I'm not sure what motivates them, or why they chose to follow Clarke and protect him, but they did, okay? There's a reason they're here."

Just then Adam's phone rang. He answered it on speaker, glaring at Wilson. "What?"

"Is this the head of IronClad Security?"

"It is. I'm a bit busy, who's calling?"

"This is General Malden, U.S. Army. I won't keep you, but I understand you've been in contact with one of my associates, a Colonel Anderson."

"Yes, Sir. He heads a private group assisting me with the security—"

"I'm aware of his role. It seems he's misappropriated some military assets resulting in some inconveniences to my department. Could you pass along that it's imperative he contact me immediately?"

"Sure, Sir, but why don't you contact him yourself, directly?"

"Do you have a direct line to him?"

"Of course I do. You don't?"

"His usual channels of communication seem to have been compromised."

"I'll give you the number I have." He rattled it off from memory. "I really do need to get to work here, Sir."

"No problem, thank you."

The call ended and Wilson gave him a look. "What do you think now?"

A moment of silence stretched as Adam rubbed his chin. "I think we need to re- check some things."

"What did he do for you so far?"

"A secondary screening of the stage area and the floor for explosives."

"What?"

"I know. We did it once, but he had the new electronic "sniffers" and I figured it wouldn't hurt to have his men search too."

"I'm sure they found nothing."

"That's what he said."

Wilson glanced at his watch. "This kicks off at seven?"

"That's the schedule."

"Give me a few men, and stall."

"I don't have a few men."

"Free some up. I'm going down to look around, and hopefully to find Clarke."

"Clarke is here?"

"You can arrest him later, even collect your reward, but for now, I need him and the cooperation of any of your men you can spare. We need to check the floor and stage again."

"Here's an extra ID If you find Clarke, give it to him. It will get him around with as little harassment as I can guarantee. If someone recognizes him..."

"I got it."

Adam picked up a radio. "Attention all units, we have a situation."

That was all Wilson heard before he was out the door and making his way toward the stage as quickly as possible.

————

"ANDERSON."

"Anderson, it's Malden."

"General. How did you get this number?"

"Unimportant. Seems you've been busy."

"Yes, Sir, I have."

"You are hereby ordered to report for duty immediately, your leave is hereby revoked. You will present yourself at Gowen Field prepared for escorted transport. Be ready to answer some questions, a lot of them. You've stepped too far over the line this time, Colonel. You are in deep shit. Your ass is mine, and it will be thoroughly inspected, and your head removed before it's fucked. Do you hear me, soldier?"

It had been a long time since anyone had dressed him down that way. No one had both the rank and the balls. The operation was headed south, and he might be able to save it, or he could lick his wounds, head home and take his punishment, which although he knew would be significant would be carried out in private. The armed forces would not want the news of the embarrassment of an officer of his rank to reach the public. Maybe he could make a deal.

"I'm waiting, Colonel." The words cut through his thoughts. Fish or cut bait. Jump forward or jump back.

"With all due respect, General, fuck you. I'm out."

"Your ass is the property of the U.S. Government. You can't quit. It doesn't work that way."

"It does today. Fuck off."

He threw the phone to the ground and stomped on it.

Dale looked at him. "Problem, Colonel?" A little smug smile tugged at the corners of his mouth.

"Fuck you." The Colonel punched him in the face. There were only a few people who had that cell number. One was Adam. If Malden had tracked him here, there was no escape for him. He'd just told his most superior officer to fuck off.

This operation was the only thing he had left, the only thing he could control and make right. He couldn't do it from across the river. Even now they might be re-checking for explosives if he and his men weren't trusted any more.

He regretted stomping on the phone now. It was his contact with the snipers. "Give me your phone," he yelled to a nearby man.

An aging cell was thrust into his hands, but it would do. Entering a number, he keyed a text: *Go. Forward.*

Anderson tossed the phone over his shoulder, and the man who'd handed it to him scrambled for it.

Fuck him, too. Fuck them all.

He pulled his pistol and yelled at the top of his lungs: "Whoever wants to finish this thing, follow me!"

Firing a shot into the air, he strode forward. A dog stepped in front of him, baring its teeth and growling. He shot it between the eyes and the body dropped to the ground. Another mutt stepped in to take its place, and he shot that one too.

The night erupted in gunshots as the other men got the idea.

A full dozen dogs died before the rest got the idea and scattered.

The bridge sidewalk was deserted, and they crossed in eerie silence, the rush of the river below the only sound.

They moved as a group across the parking area, eliciting a few stares from the people still milling around, but they dismissed them as another part of the tight security present for this most momentous of evenings.

Whenever a dog even approached him and his men, someone

fired. The dogs either backed off or died. He smiled. It would be a historical night. A night long remembered.

———

LIMPING, I glimpsed the stage from time to time, saw the thousands filling in the chairs, the bleachers. Something sinister tainted the air, and I couldn't tell what it was yet. Under almost every set of bleachers, I glimpsed a tail, an ear, or a pair of eyes. The dogs were gone from outside. I could hear passersby talking about it, but there were still dogs in the shadows, besides the two that led us. They seemed to be waiting for something.

We came around a corner into a well-lit area, and the dogs stopped, growling. As I struggled forward, I looked up to see another armed guard. He stared back at us, saw the blood on my leg, and pulled his weapon, leaving it lowered at his side. The dogs growled at his advance.

"Evening folks," he said, his tone polite on the surface, but hard and alert underneath. "You can't have dogs in here, especially after what happened earlier. You understand, right?" He smiled, watching our every movement.

"Dogs? These aren't our dogs. We got turned around back there looking for our seats, and we just happened on them. Can you help us?" Marsha stalled well, but it was just that, a stall. With no tickets, our story wouldn't hold up. I searched desperately for something that would help.

"Sure," he said, still watchful. "It looks like you got hurt there, Sir. Did that happen this evening? Can I get you some medical assistance?"

Following his gaze, I realized what a mess my leg had become. It had closed up crudely earlier, but all the activity and the fight had opened it again. My pants were tattered and stained with blood. Even the tops of my shoes showed evidence of trauma.

My mind worked on an excuse, no matter how lame. Then I saw Wilson behind the guard.

"Stand down," he said. "These two are with me." He produced a badge, and the guard stepped back.

"Who are you?" he asked.

"A friend of your boss. You can call him and ask him questions if you want, but I need this man to help me with an urgent security issue."

"He looks injured, Sir."

"He is, but he's the only one who can help. There is about to be an incident, and he can help prevent it."

I looked at my watch. Six forty-five. Fifteen minutes until show time, and we still didn't know the Colonel's plan. If his previous MOs were any indication, he'd be long gone, and any clues to his involvement carefully erased before anyone pieced together what happened.

The guard looked like he might argue with Wilson more, but then we all heard gunshots from near one of the gates. An inhuman scream pierced the evening air, and all conversation in the stands stopped.

"What was that?" a man asked.

More gunshots followed, and the guard turned and ran toward them. The two dogs leading us barked urgently and took off toward the stage. I struggled to keep up.

"Should we evacuate?" someone yelled.

Wilson turned and projected his voice with former drill instructor authority: "No! Stay in your seats. Security will assist you shortly."

Anderson didn't mind collateral damage, but he wouldn't create any more than he had to. At least, that had been true at one time.

The gunfire outside told me that the Colonel, or at least his men were still here. Maybe he was all-in on this operation.

I limped along as fast as I could. Some of the civilians stood and tried to leave. I shoved them out of the way, struggling to keep my balance, in severe pain, my vision blurring.

Twenty feet from the stage I saw Sparky's head poke out from underneath. He barked at me, and I hurried faster.

Ten feet. Five.

A bee stung on my already bad thigh, and a second later I heard the soft whisper of a silenced rifle from above and behind me. Falling forward, barely catching myself and lowering my body to the ground, I discovered my leg was useless. Sparky was nose to nose with me. He barked and darted under the stage, looking back.

Follow me, I heard as he moved quickly ahead.

Ignoring the pain the best I could, I crawled forward. A second later I felt a form beside me, and Marsha was there, crawling too. She moved faster than me, and soon I could see her and Sparky stop ahead. Moving as fast as possible, I heard the sounds of crowd panic erupt around the stage, and then from overhead like the voice of God, Wilson's amplified voice surrounded me.

"Stop! Take your seats. We'll get you out of here, but we need you to remain calm and exit in an orderly manner."

"Fuck you!" I heard faintly.

From directly above me, a gunshot sounded. "Orderly, I said."

The crowd noise calmed to a murmur, and I turned my attention to Sparky and Marsha. Something gray and shaped like a cone sat directly in front of him, mounted to what would be the floor of the stage. Six wires ran from the material to a clock on the side that read 8:10. An antenna stuck out of the center of the timer.

"Can you disarm it?" Marsha asked.

I nodded, but I knew there would be others. This one was targeted to take out the speaker.

Eight minutes, and the antenna told me there was a remote. If Anderson got spooked, he could set it off sooner.

"Sparky," I said, looking him in the eye. "Are there more?

Find them, boy." He barked once and waited. I knew what he meant.

There were more, and he knew where they were. This one was just first. I got to work studying the mechanism, sweat from the suffocating heat and the trauma of the injury running into my eyes, doubling my vision.

"Todd." Marsha said, and I saw she was crying. I followed her gaze and saw that the blood was leaving my leg in a river.

"Tourniquet."

"But you need—"

"After," I told her, indicating the bomb. "They'll never get everyone out in time." She got to work on my leg, and I felt her movements down there as I studied the device, pulling first one wire, then the next. Slowly, I removed the detonator from the brick of explosive.

I felt my belt leave my pants, and then felt it tighten around my thigh. I screamed in pain, and from above I heard a gasp.

"Time to move." I felt weak, but I had to keep going. She crawled up beside me and pulled me along as Sparky led us to the next bomb.

––––––––

"STOP FIRING! Goddamn it, which one of you bastards pulled that trigger? You're giving away your position. We have two primary targets! Two! Only fire if you see them unless you get other orders. Understood?"

The answer came back a muffled "Yes, Sir."

"The targets will be in the green room. The back-stage area. Team One, with me. The rest of you, fan out and secure the limo, the chopper, and the perimeter. Don't let Reverend Wolfe or that fucking Governor out of here."

A dozen men followed him as he rounded the building and the rest fanned out. "The dogs?" A soldier asked.

"If you feel threatened, shoot to kill."

"Yes, Sir."

Security would be moving, relocating the targets. Up ahead, he heard voices and the sound of men scrambling around.

"Get him out!" The shout floated to his ears over the chaos. He motioned to his men, and they started to run.

A second later, a pair of guards appeared in the hallway ahead. They turned, spotting the threat. The first dropped to a crouch, the second slid back, using the corner for cover, and they opened fire. A bullet whizzed past the Colonel's ear, and he heard a grunt behind him. The rest of the shots went over their heads.

Moving to the wall, he returned fire, aiming low and left with his first shot. His second was right on, and the crouching man flew backward and lay still. The other fled.

One of his men sagged against the wall with a gaping wound in his shoulder. "Jensen, tend to him. The rest of you, let's go."

The element of surprise, if there had been any, was gone. Speed was the new priority.

———

"He wasn't on the phone long enough, General."

"Give me a fucking idea, soldier. Where do you think he is?"

"Sir!" Another soldier approached from the left, a tremor in his voice. He came to attention and saluted. The General returned a half-assed salute rapidly.

"Knock off the bullshit, soldier, and spit it out if it's important enough."

"The local police, Sir. They reported shots fired at the rally downtown."

"Shots fired?"

"They report a military-type force breaching. They're moving the Governor and Reverend Wolfe now."

"How soon can you get me there?"

"Twenty minutes, Sir," the other soldier answered. "Chopper?"

"From here, it would be faster by ground. By the time we fuel and ready a chopper crew—"

"Give me your fastest fucking driver, and your best Hummer. If he gets me there in ten, he's promoted. Understood?"

"Yes, Sir!" Both soldiers saluted and scampered from sight.

———

FROM THE STAGE, Wilson spotted the glint of light off a scope. The guy had picked a perfect perch. Too perfect. No one would think to look there except for someone else looking for a perfect perch. He'd seen Clarke hit, seen him and Marsha disappear under the stage following Sparky, suspected why, and there wasn't a thing he could do for them now. The density of the crowd would've prevented him from moving that way, even if he wanted to.

No, he'd be better off trying to find the rest of the assailants. His sidearm, a 9mm Smith and Wesson with an extended clip held fifteen rounds. He wished for a rifle or even a short barrel shotgun right now. If wishes were weapons, soldiers would always triumph.

He crossed himself, a move remembered from his Catholic school days long ago, and couldn't help but chant "Spectacles, testicles, wallet and watch" under his breath. As he turned to search for a back way up top, a dog appeared at his feet. The graying mutt with spots of black and tan tangled fur barked up at him, and he understood.

Follow me, the look said.

He trotted off after the hairy tail, struggling to keep up.

———

Annabelle nearly ran into Bobbie coming out of the door. "You again? Didn't you hear the shots? Get out of here!"

"I want to help." Bobbie stood her ground, and behind the other woman a security officer appeared, gun in hand.

"Move ma'am," he said simply.

"Whoever is after you knows where you're headed. I have another idea."

"Who's this, Anna?" The Reverend Benjamin Wolfe joined his wife, and the security officer tensed.

"She's a reporter, Ben, and—"

"Look, yes, I am a reporter, but I came here with a couple guys who are trying to stop whatever is happening. I can help you."

"We're wasting time, Sir." The security man said anxiously.

"I can help," Bobbie Ann insisted.

A shot sounded from down the corridor, and the whine of a ricochet terminated in a sick thud. The security officer dropped his gun and slid to the floor.

Benjamin stared, and Annabelle put her hand to her mouth.

"He was right, we're wasting time. Duck, and follow me," Bobbie said.

Her voice sounded so confident, but she felt far from it. She had no idea where Clarke or Wilson were, and she had no training. But she knew where they'd parked the SUV, and that it was full of weapons.

The Governor slid out beside them. "I'm with you."

As she spoke, another dark-suited officer stepped into the hall. A shot sounded and he fell.

It spurred the men to action. Benjamin grabbed Annabelle's elbow, and all they followed Bobbie as she sprinted down the corridor. As she ran, she saw two dogs run her way, Doberman mixes. They bolted past her toward the gunfire.

She didn't stop to think about what they were doing and went on. She slowed and the Governor passed her, his breath coming in panicked gasps. "Wait!" She called after him, but he wasn't seeing anything right now, just running.

A moment later she heard barking and growling.

Another group of a half dozen dogs flew past, and she turned to watch them go. As she did, the Reverend tripped and fell. Annabelle dropped to the ground next to him.

Bobbie ran back to her.

"Anna, go!" he said. His leg looked...well, wrong. His ankle looked out of joint. "Ben, no!"

"Go!"

Bobbie grabbed her arm and pulled her along.

"We'll get help, and send it for him," she said, not believing it herself. Annabelle sobbed, but kept up.

———

I COULDN'T SEE. Everything was blurry. There were two Marshas, two Sparkys, two bombs, four yellow wires, and two timers reading 1:00.

:59

:58

:57

Wiped my sleeve across my eyes. Gunshots, distant. Marsha, pale.

"You can do it," she said. Her voice shook, I think. Or my hearing shook.

A bark. Sparky. Good dog.

My hands shook. I couldn't. I had to.

:29

:28

:27

God, if you're there, help me now. Jesusamenamen.

:19

Pulled one wire. Unclip. Steady. Easy.

:12

Wire two. Fumbled. Dropped. Grabbed again. Unclip. Damn, that thing is strong. Strong. I was weak.

:06

:05

Got it.

Marsha smiled, Sparky wagged his tail.

Good boy. I did it.

We made it.

I heard a blast. Distant.

Oops, missed one, I thought.

A flash of light. Crushing, crushing weight. Blackness. Ah, sweet relief from pain.

Dove, swimming through the dark, toward a bright, deep blue light. Then nothing.

CHAPTER TWENTY

"**S**hoot them!"

The dogs split up, and bullets careened off the floor, missing their targets. Teeth flashed, barks sounded.

Anderson spun to the side and hugged the wall, wanting to choose his shots wisely.

The lead dog lunged past him, and one of his team moved forward to meet him, foolishly shooting too high. The bullet whizzed down the corridor, and the dog leapt. The soldier raised his forearm to protect himself, and teeth sunk in, tearing flesh.

The Colonel turned in time to see the other dog coming for him. It snarled and sunk its teeth into his calf. The pain was excruciating, and he roared. Bringing his pistol around, he shot the dog in the head. The jaws released, and it fell still.

Another canine moved on to the next soldier, but he was better prepared. He dodged the first assault and spun, his movement confined by the small area. The soldier behind him fired at the dog and missed. The bullet chipped the wall tile and bounced off the concrete floor underneath. It struck the first bitten soldier in his knee, blowing it apart.

"Cease fire, you fuck!" Colonel Anderson yelled, but both soldiers were now engaged with the dog as it circled and snarled, the battle trapping the other soldiers behind them. The dog saw an opening and shot forward, grabbing the crotch of the second man. He screamed, his eyes suddenly wide with shock.

The first soldier kicked out at the dog. A whimper escaped its throat, but still its jaws held, despite the loud crack of breaking bone. He raised his pistol, butt first, and struck the dog in the head once, twice, and a third time before the dog fell to the floor, alive but panting heavily, eyes glazed. The bitten soldier sunk to the floor, blood soaking the front of his pants and forming a puddle underneath him.

The rest of the unit poured through the opening, racing in front of him. The Colonel sagged against the wall for a moment, winded and perplexed. What the hell was up with all of these dogs, and why were they protecting Ben? He looked at the two wounded soldiers. Both were breathing raggedly. The one with the mangled crotch lay on the floor, unconscious. If he didn't get help soon, he would bleed out.

Anderson pushed off the wall. He had to end this, and hope he'd find help in time. Men were dying, and he didn't want it to be for nothing.

Men like Reverend Wolfe, men like the new Governor, they didn't belong here, especially in positions of leadership. They were what was wrong with the military, the government, and now his home state. They needed to be reminded, to be put back where they belonged.

He stumbled forward, cursing as he heard more barking and growling from up ahead.

———

THE DOG RAN the stairs like an Olympian, and Wilson struggled behind.

Jesus, that dog is quick.

A figure slipped down the side of the press box, a rifle slung over its shoulder.

He's seen us coming, and he's running. Us?

It was insane, thinking of himself and a dog as a team, but he did. The man turned, a large pistol in his hand. The dog launched at him. The man didn't fire but pulled his forearm up to protect himself. Canine jaws closed on his exposed flesh and he grimaced in pain, a roar echoing off the concrete walls.

Wilson drew his weapon, pointing it at the man's head. "Down, boy!" The dog let go and stood at heel, waiting.

The man dropped his weapon, gripping his wounded arm with his other hand. "Who are you?"

"What do you mean?"

"You. All these fucking dogs. Who are you guys? Why are you protecting these guys man?"

"I don't know what you mean."

He started to laugh. Clearly, it was painful at first, but then he laughed harder, sliding to a sitting position on the closest step. Wilson kept him covered, suspicious.

"You're tellin' me you don't even know what's going on here?"

"Not really. Just that my friend Clarke got mixed up in this, and a Colonel Anderson—"

"Colonel Anderson? Seriously?"

"Yeah. He's some kind of white supremacist—"

Blood ran down his arm and pooled between his feet, and still he guffawed. The sniper released the pressure on the wound, and for a moment blood spurted, but he pulled up his sleeve. "You see that?"

Three numbers decorated his bicep, wrapped in intricate designs and thorny vines, but readable. 12, 14, 88. "You know what that means?"

Wilson looked behind him, and then down at the dog at his side. The pooch faced backward, inches from his knee, eyes alert and watchful. "No, but I suspect it means you're an Aryan too."

"A member of the supreme race. An expression of God's will for humanity. So you're about to kill perfection personified. You're interrupting God's work!"

A dull boom sounded from the stadium floor, and Wilson turned in time to see the stage tilt and fall at an angle onto one corner. A cloud of dust rose, obscuring his view. What remained of the crowd collectively screamed, and controlled panic rapidly turned into a stampede. The exits clogged with humanity, and wails of pain joined those of surprise, fear, and anguish as bodies were pressed and trampled in a frantic scramble for freedom.

Laughter came from behind him, and Wilson turned, angry.

"Anderson is just a pawn. Hell, so am I. You'll never stop the Cause. Even if we fail today, we will not be swept under the rug. It's time for a revolution."

"You're right about one thing. Not today." Wilson raised his pistol and shot the man in the center of his forehead.

He turned away looking for a path to the floor of the stadium, looking for a way to reach his friends. The dog beside him barked and tugged at his sleeve. Wilson didn't know the way, so he followed. As he ducked to enter the corridor the dog chose, he saw movement on the floor below. A dust-covered Sparky emerged and climbed painfully to the tilted stage. A howl of anguish and longing filled the space, echoing off the walls, carrying far into the night.

A sharp bark from the dog ahead broke his momentary paralysis, and he trotted behind him, hoping beyond hope that Clarke was not...

He held on to that hope.

———

Colonel Anderson heard the boom and stopped. The dogs silenced for a moment. The boom wasn't big enough, but it was something.

A distraction. all he needed, he broke into a limping awkward sprint. Ahead, the dogs and men were engaged in an immobile standoff, looking inward as if they could see through the walls, trying to figure out the source of the explosion. His invasion of their space returned time to normal speed, and one of the dogs turned toward him with a snarl.

Familiar fear rose in his throat, but he didn't hesitate. He grabbed the closest man by the collar, and threw him toward the dog. The animal dodged, and the Colonel limped around the fallen man, barely clearing him. The dog lunged after his fleeing form. The fallen soldier reached out, grabbing its tail. Turning, it sunk its teeth into the soft flesh of his hand. He cried out, striking out with a booted foot. The fight freed the other men and dogs and they circled each other, looking for openings. The Colonel raced around the corner and slid to a stop.

Propped against the wall sat Benjamin, clearly in pain, jaw set. He looked up. "Hello Mike."

"Hi Ben."

"What's all this? Surely it's not just for me."

"No, you were just the start. You triggered this in me, inspired it, you could say."

"Triggered? How?"

"You remember high school, right? I was the best, the captain of the football team, the basketball team. Then you came along."

"Mike, high school?"

"Yeah. My father taught me right. We are superior to folks like...well, like you."

"You mean racially." Benjamin shifted, and Colonel Anderson smiled. The man looked uncomfortable and nervous. Good.

"Yes. You came in and took over. You didn't notice how we looked at you? How we hated you?"

"I did. I just didn't care. I moved on."

"So did I. Then it happened again. In the Army. Some fuck like you named Colbert. Tried to show me how much better he was. Tried to be superior."

"Mike, what's the point?"

"The point is I decided to do something about it. I stayed in. Served my country. Rose in the ranks. Did my time in the trenches. Found there were others who felt like I did. Built a unit, and as they left, kept in touch with some. The elite. The Aryans. Some of them formed a group that calls itself the Cause. My Cause."

"Your Cause?"

"To return you to your rightful place, at my feet, like where you are now."

Anderson raised his pistol. "I've been waiting for this for years, Ben. It's personal, but not personal. You're not even a person. This is just like shooting a dog," he glanced down at Ben's swelling leg. "A dog or even a horse with a broken leg. Putting it out of its misery."

————

WILSON ROUNDED the corner and saw something really strange.

Reverend Wolfe, who resembled his photos only vaguely, sat on the floor, propped against a wall, one leg out in front of him. Across from him stood a large man in civilian-type clothing pointing a large pistol at the Reverend's chest.

Wilson heard the words "putting it out of its misery" as he slid to a stop. The dog didn't stop. He flew through the air, striking the towering man in the chest. As he turned, Wilson recognized him. Colonel Anderson.

He batted the dog away, and as it rolled down the corridor, he aimed at it and fired. His first shot missed.

"No!" Wilson screamed and moved to attack when the gun swung back around. The barrel pointed right between his eyes.

"Who are you? You look familiar."

"Why do you want to know?"

"I like to keep track of the men I've killed by name."

Benjamin crept forward as if to grab his leg, but the Colonel saw the movement and kicked him square in the chest without flinching. The Reverend slid back to the wall, breathing heavily.

"Wait your turn, Ben. Now you. Who are you, and why are you here?"

"I'm a friend of Clarke's and—"

A snarl came from behind him, and Wilson stopped.

The Colonel looked over Wilson's shoulder.

"Tsk, tsk. I don't know why these dogs are helping you, protecting you, but I've never liked dogs, and I'm getting tired of killing them."

A head brushed his hand, and Wilson looked down. Sparky gave him a doggie smile decorated with a panting tongue, and then turned his attention to the Colonel, whose gun was pointed right at the dog, his head tilted in recognition. "Is this your dog? He looks familiar."

"I don't know whose he is," Wilson answered honestly.

"Well, that's a shame." Anderson pulled the trigger, but Sparky was no longer there.

Sparky bit Anderson's calf, then let it go and darted away. The Colonel fired again, missing, and Wilson jumped at his back, shoving him as hard as he could. Anderson fell to his knees and brought the gun back around, this time pointing it at Ben instead.

"Back off, fucker. Or I kill him."

"He's going to kill me anyway," Ben said.

Even Sparky hesitated, unwilling to move. His tail wagged, indicating a deep understanding.

"You're right," Anderson said.

"Mike," Ben said, and time slowed down.

Colonel Anderson's finger tightened on the trigger. Sparky moved, striking his shooting arm from underneath, sending the shot high. Wilson dove for his feet.

You hit him high, I'll hit him low, he thought. Then his shoulder struck the larger man's knees, and he heard a crack. Pain radiated down his arm, and suddenly he wasn't sure if the noise had been the snap of his shoulder or the Colonel's leg breaking.

The Colonel toppled to the left, and the gun flew from his

hand. Sparky landed lightly on his hind legs, spun, and sprinted, mouth open, catching the gun before it struck the ground. He took it, not to Wilson, but to Benjamin.

The Reverend removed the gun gently from the dog's mouth and pointed it at Colonel Anderson.

"It seems the tables have turned, Mike," he said.

———

THE TIRES SQUEALED as General Malden's vehicle skidded into the parking lot. The area was a disaster. There was a sea of faces running from the stadium. Police and SWAT officers tried to control the panic, but it clearly wasn't working. Private security forces mixed with them, most staying close to the structure, needlessly blocking exits to keep anyone from re-entering.

No one seemed to be in charge, but the driver the base had assigned him did not disappoint. By his watch, they'd made it here in twelve minutes, and the soldier honked and pushed ahead, forcing the crowds out of the way, surmising correctly that the General would want to be dropped front and center.

The Hummer reached the main entrance at the south end of the stadium. "Who's in charge here?" he asked the security officer.

"IronClad Security."

"Adam?"

"Yes, Sir."

"You have a radio?"

"Yes, Sir." He handed it over. Good. Ex-military, and still ingrained enough that when an officer stepped in, he followed orders.

Malden turned away, keying the mike. "Everyone on this net, this is General Malden, U.S. Army. Secure all entrances. No one in or out." He let the key go, debating what else to say, and looked around.

Walking toward him was a man in a bike helmet, hands clearly cuffed behind his back.

"Sergeant Fischer?" he asked.

"General. I'd salute, but—"

"Officer!" he called. "Uncuff this man."

The officer complied, and Dale rubbed his wrists.

"What's going on, Dale?"

"I may be able to shed some light on that, Sir. Do you know Colonel Mike Anderson?"

"Yes, unfortunately."

"He's the one who coordinated at least part of this party. A Todd Clarke tried to stop it."

"Clarke?"

"Yes, Sir."

"How did you get involved?"

"His men killed some of my friends and my dog."

"Your dog?"

"Sir, we can talk about that later. They captured me. The Colonel suspected my motives and locked me up. They forgot me on the other side of the river when they came over. Something went wrong, and it has to do with all these dogs."

The General looked around. Mixed in with all of the people were dozens of dogs, all breeds and sizes. Some sat in the door-ways, as if guarding them. Some sat in the shadows, watchful. Some mingled with the crowd, who seemed to hardly notice them except for occasionally patting their heads.

Where they were present, the crowd, now just staring curiously at the stadium, was calmer.

"Are you hurt?" he asked Dale.

"No, Sir. Stiff, but not hurt."

"Come with me." The General strode past the guard, who made no move to stop the pair, and they entered the concrete structure. It smelled of sweat, fear, gunpowder, and smoke.

They reached the floor of the stadium, and saw the stage tilted to one side, dust surrounding it on the floor. At the corner still most supported, they saw two forms. Dale rushed forward, the General close on his heels.

A woman lay next to Clarke. He was pale and appeared to be barely breathing. The woman sobbed.

"He won't wake up. He won't wake up." She kept repeating. The General turned and yelled. "Medic! We need a medic here." No one moved, anywhere. A rustling came from mid-level of the stadium, but no one came toward them.

He keyed the radio still in his hand. "All on this band, I need EMTs and assistance on the stadium floor, now."

"Copy that." Came a faint answer.

Dale knelt by the woman, and saw her legs and Clarke's were both pinned under some of the fallen structure. "What's your name?"

"Marsha," she said. "Please help him."

"Marsha?" The General knelt. "I'm General Malden. Your husband and I know each other. Help is on the way. We'll take care of him, I promise."

Dale looked at him. "You served with Clarke?"

"You could say that. You two did similar work."

The General smiled and looked around. It was quiet in the stadium now, but he heard new sirens, and scanned the entrances, looking for the promised help. Then from the east side, he heard a gunshot followed by a man screaming.

———

THE GUN WENT OFF. Anderson screamed.

Wilson looked. No gaping wound spurted blood, no air escaped the Colonel's chest. His breath came in fearful gasps, his limbs were all whole.

"I'm not like you," Ben said. " None of us are superior or inferior. None."

"Come here, Sparky," he said. The dog obeyed. "Look at him, Colonel. You think he would enslave the poodle? Tell the Shih

Tzu that it is less than he because of its parentage? No. Dogs have alphas when they run in packs, but the determining factor in who leads is not breed or heritage. It is strength, agility, wisdom. The ability to find food, and to provide. Even the ability to breed."

"You make me sick," the Colonel spat out the words.

"Help me up," Benjamin asked Wilson.

He moved over, lifting the Reverend to his feet. He kept the gun trained on Anderson the whole time.

The Colonel moved, and Sparky growled.

"Easy boy," Ben soothed.

"So what now?"

"I have a speech to make. Sir, can you get me to the stage?"

Wilson's shoulder was on fire. He looked at Benjamin's ankle. It looked swollen, probably a bad sprain, but didn't appear to be broken. "I think so. Call me Wilson. Everyone else does. What about him?"

He gestured with the pistol. "Go ahead, Colonel. Stay in front of us until we get out of here. I want you to have a front row seat."

The Colonel reluctantly stood and took the lead, limping. Wilson helped the Reverend limp forward as well. Whenever the Colonel got too far ahead, Sparky growled and barked, and he slowed. They walked down a ramp, and turned a corner, struggling toward the center of the stadium. A large, older man in uniform with three stars on his shoulders moved toward them.

"Colonel," he said.

"General," the Colonel saluted, shoulders sagging.

"You're finished." The General said.

Colonel Anderson spun then, and tried for the gun. Reverend Benjamin Wolfe pulled the trigger.

A red blotch appeared in the center of the Colonel's chest, and he fell to his knees. The gun went off again.

Again. And again.

The Colonel's body fell forward. The Reverend fired again, causing the body to twitch as a hole appeared in its back.

The gun clicked once, twice, three times as Ben kept pulling the trigger even though he was out of ammunition. Suddenly they were surrounded, security forces and police propelling them outside.

Through the crowd, he saw some EMTs and firemen clustered around a corner of the stage, cutting metal.

Sparky broke away and ran towards them.

———

I HEARD A BUZZING, buzzing, buzzing, and my head hurt.

Jesus, someone shut that shit up.

It let up for a second, and then started again. I heard a whimper, and voices.

What does a guy have to do to get some sleep around here? Where am I?

I listened. Voices in my head usually filled let me know what was happening when I awoke from these combat-induced fugues.

There was combat, wasn't there? There was something.

A dog barked, and I was glad.

Glad? Why?

"Todd! Oh, Todd, are you with us?"

Marsha's voice as the buzzing stopped. I felt something lifted from me.

I was trapped. Was I?

Hands on me. Their touch hurt, comforted. I tried to answer. "Yes, I'm here."

It came out as a mere groan. My vocal chords wouldn't work, my voice was gone.

"Oh, Todd! I love you! I love you," I heard her say.

I heard two barks, and felt fur on my skin, and it felt right. So right.

"Your Honor, new evidence has come to light."

"I understand, Mr. Rockford. Mr. Jeffers?"

"Due to the usual circumstances we'd like to release Mr. Clarke on his own recognizance until the outcome of his appeal has been finalized."

"He fled once before."

"We're sure that's no longer a risk, your honor."

I watched like it was a tennis match. It was my fate, not a ball they batted back and forth. Marsha grabbed my hand, and I smiled at her. The only one missing was Sparky.

"It's on you. So ordered. Now to the contempt charges."

Three young men stood, dressed in shirts and ties that clearly made them uncomfortable.

"You gentlemen are accused of lying under oath in this case, giving false testimony. How do you plead?"

"Mr. Johnson for the defense your Honor. We'd like to enter a plea of guilty."

"Is this part of a plea deal with the prosecution?"

"Yes, your Honor."

"Mr. Jeffers?"

"Due to the circumstances, your Honor, we request supervised probation until each of the boys turn 21."

"And what are these circumstances Mr. Jeffers?"

"We believe these juveniles were compelled by someone in authority who they trusted to give false testimony."

"They are also being tried as adults in a separate case related to the initial accident they lied about, correct?"

"Yes, your Honor."

"Then this court will withhold its verdict on this matter until the outcome of that trial is known. Until that time, the boys are ordered to remain in the custody of the State of Idaho in an appropriate correctional facility."

"Thank you, your Honor." The gavel pounded the bench, and we moved to leave. I saw Mr. Johnson talking to the boys. He shook their hands, they exited, and he walked over.

"Mr. Clarke," he said, shaking my hand. "Pleased to meet you. I'm Samuel Johnoson. You can call me Sam."

"Marsha," he shook my wife's hand. I noticed a gold band on his left ring finger that looked new.

"Good work Rockford."

"Sam is kind of my boss," Rockford explained.

"So what'll happen to the kids?" I asked.

"They'll get the best defense we can give them. They did the wrong thing, but at least they finally told the truth."

"Good. If we can help financially or anything—" Marsha said.

He held up his hand. "No need. Good luck you two."

We walked out of the courtroom, and for the first time in years, I felt like a truly free man.

"Let's go home." Marsha led me out into the light. She drove as we headed north, well out of town.

———

Dale Fischer stood outside his offices, conflicted. The sign read "closed until further notice".

It'd been that way for nearly three months. It was time.

His brow furrowed with indecision. Men were dead because of his decisions. Lives had been forever altered. He'd gone to four funerals, and then stopped going.

He had a choice. Move forward, change, grow. Or crawl into a hole.

Placing the key in the lock, he turned it. Opened the door. The place smelled of mold and neglect. Dust covered everything.

He opened the front window first, and then moved into the office. Stared at the phone. The computer.

Listened. Kids playing across the street in the park. Dogs barking.

Dogs barking.

He sat down hard in his chair. Putting his head in his hands, he sobbed.

Minutes passed, and he stopped, looking up. Sun played with the swirling air, and he switched on the stand fan in the corner, sending more dirt flying.

On his desk, in a small frame, was a picture of him and his Lab, a shotgun in his hand, a duck in Ricky's mouth. A bag of decoys lay at his feet.

Maybe he couldn't do this after all. The bell over his door rang.

Wiping his eyes, he moved to the front office. Wilson stood there, with another man in tow.

"Hi Dale."

"Wilson. What are you doing here?'

"Came to offer you a job."

"A job?"

"Well, he did actually." Wilson gestured at the man following him.

"Adam, IronClad security," the man introduced himself. "I'm forming a new unit in my company, and I think you're the man to head it up."

"A new unit?"

"K-9."

Dale drew in a deep breath. "I'm not sure..." A scratching sounded at the door.

"The job comes with a new partner," Wilson said with a grin, and opened it. A tiny black puppy scampered in, claws seeking purchase on the slick tile. He ran right up and jumped in Dale's lap, licking his face.

Dale laughed. It was too soon. It had been too long. It hadn't been long enough. It never would be long enough.

"Hi, Little Richard," he said.

"Little Richard?" Wilson laughed.

"There will never be another Ricky. I accept. Does this mean we'll be working together Wilson?"

He nodded.

"Give me a minute would you?"

Wilson and Adam left. Little Richard scampered around Dale's feet as he packed a box, piling in the laptop and the few files he wanted to take with him. The rest could wait. He turned the old picture face down on the desk and walked out.

"RAY, HOW ARE YOU DOING?"

"Feeling better. You, Sheriff?"

"Okay. Did you hear about the compound?"

"The one they blew up in the middle of all that crazy shit six weeks ago?"

"Yeah. Someone bought it."

"Really? Who would do that?"

"Don't know, but they must have money. How's the dog?"

"All right. Travis seems to have recovered from his little adventure, wherever he went."

"Good to hear." Sheriff Crawford rubbed the fur on the dog's head, sure to scratch behind his ears the way he liked. "I should get going. Just thought I would check in since I was up this way."

"Thanks."

As he turned to go, there was a knock on the door. Travis nearly bowled him off his feet, barking and rushing for it.

"You expecting anyone?"

"No," Ray said, rising painfully to his feet.

Alma walked in behind them. "Who's that?" she asked.

"Don't know yet, dear. The kryptonite screwed with my x-ray vision, so I have to open the door first."

"Knock off the smart-ass Ray."

"Yes dear," he said, and the Sheriff followed him as he limped to the door.

Ray opened it. Clarke stood on the doorstep with a beautiful woman beside him. Travis rushed out, and he and Sparky wrestled and barked as they rolled around on the lawn, tails wagging in greeting and friendship.

"What are you doing here?" Ray asked.

"What's wrong?" The corner of Clarke's mouth turned up in a smirk. "Can't a neighbor stop in to borrow a cup of sugar?"

Troy began his writing life at a very young age, penning the as yet unpublished George and the Giant Castle at age six. He grew up in Southern Idaho, and after many adventures including a short stint in the US Army and a diverse education, Troy returned to Idaho, and currently resides in Boise.

He works as a freelance writer, author of many mysteries, researcher, and editor. His work includes

Troy lives with his wife and a very talented German shepherd. He is a skier, cyclist, hiker, fisherman, hunter, and a terrible beginning golfer.

———

Get in touch with Troy

http://www.fictionupdates.troylambertwrites.com/
Facebook - https://www.facebook.com/authortroy/
Twitter - https://twitter.com/tlambertwrites

WHAT TO READ NEXT:

Don't miss the first exciting crime thriller in the Max Boucher series: Harvested, available on Amazon and in print.

Max Boucher is an ex-cop turned private eye. His wife is missing, his family has been killed, and he won't stop looking for her and the man who killed his family, even though everyone else has given up.

But he's been hired to investigate dogs disappearing all over Seattle. It looks like a simple case, at first, but something more sinister is going on. Something Max could have never imagined. Will he be able to find and save the dogs in time? Will the solution lead him closer to clues about his wife's whereabouts and who killed his family? You won't be able to stop reading until the very end.

The Good Shepherd, sequel to *Stray Ally*, the second in the dog complex series, is coming in 2020!

Sparky is back. A secret government agency has a plan: to use the most brilliant dogs as soldiers and spies. But the dogs, and the humans who care for them, are much smarter than expected, and now they have another agenda. Will the government end the program, and the dogs? Or will the dogs stop one of the greatest threats the nation has ever faced?

WHAT TO READ NEXT:

Coming November of 2020 from Unbound Media!